OPEN
IF YOU DARE

DANA MIDDLETON

FEIWEL AND FRIENDS

NEW YORK

A FEIWEL AND FRIENDS BOOK
An imprint of Macmillan Publishing Group, LLC
175 Fifth Avenue, New York, NY 10010

Our books may be purchased in bulk for promotional, educational, or business use. Please contact your local bookseller or the Macmillan Corporate and Premium Sales Department at (800) 221-7945 ext. 5442 or by e-mail at MacmillanSpecialMarkets@macmillan.com.

Library of Congress Cataloging-in-Publication Data

Names: Middleton, Dana, author.
Title: Open if you dare / Dana Middleton.
Description: First edition. | New York : Feiwel and Friends, 2017. | Summary: Their last summer before going to different middle schools, best friends Birdie, Ally, and Rose follow clues found in a mysterious box labeled Open If You Dare.
Identifiers: LCCN 2017002288 (print) | LCCN 2017030331 (ebook) | ISBN 9781250085733 (Ebook) | ISBN 9781250085726 (hardcover)
Subjects: | CYAC: Best friends—Fiction. | Friendship—Fiction. | Change—Fiction. | Mystery and detective stories.
Classification: LCC PZ7.1.M517 (ebook) | LCC PZ7.1.M517 Ope 2017 (print) | DDC [Fic]—dc23
LC record available at https://lccn.loc.gov/2017002288

Book design by Liz Dresner

Feiwel and Friends logo designed by Filomena Tuosto

First edition, 2017

1 3 5 7 9 10 8 6 4 2

mackids.com

To Lisa and Sally

PART 1

I TOLD YOU SO

1

"IT'S OVER!" Ally's pumping her arm in the air and yelling. "Never again!"

"Never ever," Rose adds, not as happily.

We've walked this sidewalk a thousand times. Rose, Ally, and me. Today, like way too many days, my little sister, Zora, is trailing behind us like a puppy.

"It wasn't so bad," I say, looking back at our elementary school for the last time. I mean, not the *last* last time. It's not like it's being torn down or I'm moving to Canada or anything. So, technically, I'll *see* it again. But this is the place we've spent the last five years of our lives together, and that part is over now.

"It wasn't so *good*, either," Ally says. She picks up a pinecone lying on the sidewalk and whips it at the speed limit sign halfway past the park. *BANG.* The sign quivers. As the pinecone shatters and falls to the ground, Rose whistles like she's in the bleachers watching Ally pitch.

"After we drop off Zora, you can go, right?" I ask.

"Nope," Rose replies.

I turn to her. "You have to practice today?"

"Uh-huh."

"On the last day of school?!"

"To be a great violinist," she says, imitating her mother's English accent, "one must practice each and every day." I laugh to myself. She sounds exactly like her mother when she does that. Returning to her regular American voice, she adds, "One day I'm going to launch that violin off the tallest building I can find."

"And watch your mother croak," Ally says.

"Probably."

Rose doesn't ever carry a backpack. She cradles her notebooks and folders in her arms like a teenage girl from an old movie. Her jet-black hair bounces on her shoulders and she walks down the sidewalk like she owns it.

"Birdie!" Zora grabs my arm from behind. "Can we stop?" she pleads, looking at the park and the little kids climbing on the jungle gym. "Please!"

"Not today. Mom's taking you for ice cream."

"Mom's home?" Zora asks.

"Yep. Just for you." I'm kind of lying, because it's not *just* for Zora. Mom promised to come home early from work so I could have the last day of school with my friends. Usually I have to look after Zora for the hour before Dad gets home.

CLUNK! The sound startles me. I turn to see Rose standing by the park trash can wearing her trademark *Guess what I just did* face. Her arms are utterly book-free.

"What did you do?!" I rush to the trash can and see Rose's school notebooks at the bottom of the bin. "You can't do that, Rose!"

4

"*You* can't do that," she says, her blue eyes dancing. "But it looks like *I* can."

Ally laughs and drops her backpack to the ground. As she unzips it, I stare at my little sister pointedly. "Do not look, Zora! This is very wrong." Ally pulls notebooks out of her backpack as I place my hands over Zora's seven-year-old eyes.

"Let me see! Let me see!" Zora cries.

But I don't let her see as Ally lobs her notebooks into the bin and Rose gives her a high five. At least there weren't any real books in there.

"Are we finished?" I ask. I can hear it in my voice and I know they can, too. It's my future teacher voice. Or worse, my future librarian voice.

"Yes, Miss Adams," Rose teases. But when I look at Ally, she nods a little guiltily.

"Okay, then." I take my hands off of Zora's eyes. Rose looks at me with that ridiculous grin that makes me love/hate her. "You are a terrible person," I tell her.

"I know," she says. Yeah, she *says* it, but it's not like she feels bad about it. Kinda proud, if anything. But that twinkle in her eyes cannot be denied. I laugh. She's the kind of friend you might actually jump off a cliff for.

The boys whiz by on their bikes. Way too close. Connor Gomez, Joey Wachowski, and Romeo Dawson.

"Hey!" Ally yells. "Off the sidewalk, jerk-bags!"

"Whatever, Blondie!" Joey yells back. "Broncos own this street!"

"In your dreams!"

Ally can't stand Joey Wachowski. He's her biggest pitching

competition in Little League. He pitches for the Broncos and she pitches for the Hunters. Joey thinks that baseball is no place for girls. So Ally has decided that baseball is no place for Joey Wachowski.

"Sorry!" It's Romeo who turns and smiles at us. His bike slows as the others pull ahead. Romeo has wavy hair and a nice smile. If I cared anything about boys, I would have to say that he's cute. But he's nice, too. Romeo looks at us a little too long, then pedals away to catch up with his jerk-bag friends.

I know what Rose is thinking before she says it.

"He likes me."

That's what she says every time he talks to us. And he's been talking to us more since Valentine's Day. Rose is the kind of girl Romeo should like. Cool. Popular. Ready to be liked by a boy.

"Yep," Ally agrees.

"What do you think?" Rose asks me, but I pretend not to hear. "Bird?" She groans. "Will you please grow up already?!"

"No, thanks. Boys are dumb."

Rose says, "Romeo's not."

Later, when we're sitting in a circle by the willow tree that marks the center of our island, Rose asks, "How many more days do you think we'll have like this?"

"Not enough," I answer. Tucked under the willow's shade, our knees almost touch. I've got the prime spot, leaning up against the willow's ropy bark.

"For sure not," Ally says, and shakes her head. "I guess we could count them off on a calendar."

"That would be even more depressing," Rose says, and I think she's right.

After dropping Zora off with Mom, we headed for our island but had to stop at Rose's house first. Rose lives across from the pool, around the big curve at the end of our street. Ally's house is on the other side of our school. Since her mom works, Ally comes over to our neighborhood almost every day in the summer.

On our way, Rose pulled out her phone in front of my next-door neighbors' house. "Last-day-of-school selfie!" she proclaimed, and we gathered together on the curb, posing in front of the Gillans' house. Their front yard is an actual Japanese garden with perfectly arranged plants and stones surrounding a covered koi pond. Zora loves to help our neighbor, Mrs. Gillan, feed them.

As we smiled into the phone, the Gillans' brick mailbox loomed behind us—the old metal bird on top so close it could have pecked us. Rose has a phone because . . . of course Rose has a phone. Ally has a phone, too, but just because her mom needs to know where she is. I don't have a phone yet. Maybe one day.

At Rose's house, Ally and I sat on the front porch while Rose practiced violin inside. Rose's mom (Mrs. Ashcroft to us) believes Rose has a special talent and insists she practices for at least an hour a day. Rose won't play for a minute more. At minute sixty-one, she stalked out the front door and we headed straight here.

Our island sits in the middle of the big creek that runs behind our neighborhood. To get here we have to go down the trail behind the pool, slip into the woods, take the down-stream path, and cross the tree bridge.

"What if I don't go?" Rose says, like she hasn't said this a hundred times since we found out she's moving back to England in August. It doesn't seem real that this will be our last summer together. "Doesn't she know she's ruining my life?"

I put my hand behind my back to feel for whatever's been jabbing me from the tree for the past five minutes. "She's ruining all of our lives," I say, and they don't disagree. It's funny how we seem to blame Rose's mom and not her dad, when he's the one getting transferred.

And to make things completely worse, Ally and I won't even be going to the same middle school in the fall. Because her neighborhood is on the other side of our elementary school, she'll be going to the old middle school and I'll be attending the new one. I felt so sorry for Ally when we found out she'd be the one to go it alone. But secretly, I was glad it was her, not me. Because before a month ago, when I still thought Rose was coming with me to middle school, I had yet to meet the panicky knot that is now calling my stomach home.

Ouch! What is *that sticking into me?* Turning, I look down and see a little thin wire coming through the bark near the base of the tree—which is weird because I've never noticed it before. Touching the pointy end, I jiggle it.

"Maybe I could run away," Rose says.

"Yeah, like where?" Ally asks. "To my house?"

Some bark falls away. "Or mine," I offer.

"Rather obvious, don't you think?" Rose sighs.

When I pull on the end of the wire, more bark crumples off until I realize that this wire is wrapped all the way around our tree.

"What are you doing, Bird?" Rose asks.

"Not sure." I stand up. As I draw the wire from the tree, it leads me in a circle, bark popping off with each step.

"Don't hurt our willow," Ally cautions.

The wire isn't buried that deeply into the tree. Just under the bark. So I think it's okay. After my first time around, I realize there's more. Maybe a lot more. It's like our tree has been wrapped with a spring that's holding it together.

As if reading my mind, Ally hops onto her knees and asks, "What if that wire is holding the tree up? Take away the wire and we lose our willow."

"It's not holding it up," I say unconvincingly as I unwind the second ring, revealing little grooves under the bark, like it's been here a very long time.

"It's got to be for something," says Rose. I can feel their eyes on me as I round the tree again, revealing the third ring, the freed wire trailing jaggedly behind me.

The final ring of wire is dug deeper into the bark. It's harder to pull away because over time it's become part of the tree. I force it anyway and circle to the back of the willow, to the place where we never sit.

The wire ends here, going directly into the ground. Rose and Ally appear on either side of me and we look down. "What is it?" Rose asks.

"Let's find out." I grip the wire tightly and pull. Surprisingly, it comes up much easier than I expect, sending me tumbling like a bowling pin into my friends. We land in a heap beside the tree.

"Ouch," yells Rose from the bottom.

"Sorry. Didn't expect that," I say as we scramble back to our feet.

"But look." Ally points toward the wire. It's buried about six inches deep and runs horizontally. I've exposed a couple of feet of it already. As I start to pull again, it becomes clear that the wire is leading us away from our tree.

It's been raining a lot so the earth is soft and the wire comes up easily. It's buried in a straight line.

"It's going toward the bush," Rose says, pointing at the leafy bush that marks the high point of the island.

"Who did this?" I ask, and keep pulling.

"Somebody who likes to dig," Ally answers.

"Maybe a one-eyed pirate," Rose says, and we both look at her. "What? They like to dig."

"We'll see about that," I say as the trail stops. Right at my feet. Right in front of the big bush.

"End of the line," Rose says.

"X marks the spot," says Ally. "Question mark."

"Help me." They grab the dirty wire and we all pull, but nothing happens. Releasing it, we stare at the ground. "There's something down there," I finally say.

"Yeah, probably a human skull or weird animal bones."

"Rose!" I exclaim.

"Just sayin'."

I drop to my knees and start digging with my hands. Ally joins in right away. Soon, Rose is helping, too. We don't get far. The soft topsoil yields to hard red Georgia clay. Our fingernails caked with dirt, we lean back and observe our pathetic progress.

"We need a shovel," I say.

Rose eyes Ally, the fastest runner. "There's one in the janitor's closet at the pool."

"On it," Ally says without hesitation, and takes off toward the clubhouse.

Rose and I stare at the wire that's heading toward the center of the earth and wait.

"What do you think's down there?" she asks, rubbing her chin with her dirty hands, leaving a dark splotch behind. "Really?"

"Don't know." But secretly I'm thinking: *Treasure.*

"What if there's nothing down there?" Rose says, interrupting my beautiful thought. "What if it's just a wire?"

"Why do you always do that?"

"What?"

"You know. Say it's just a wire. Why would you say that, Rose?"

"Why would I not say that? It's just a wire."

"Yeah, but somebody did this," I say. "Why would someone go to all this trouble to just bury a wire? That would be stupid."

"What do you think it is?"

"I don't know. Maybe a treasure. You know, left by a real one-eyed pi—"

"There is no one-eyed pirate!" Rose starts to laugh. Not a mean laugh but one that says she's known me for a thousand years. "That's the difference between you and me. You think there's treasure—I think there's dirt," she says. "Or bones."

She's right. That is the difference between her and me.

It's not too long before we hear footfalls crossing the tree bridge. Ally bursts onto the island, shovel in hand. "Here!" She gives me the shovel and puts her hands on her knees, breathing hard. And she hardly ever breathes hard. "What are you guys talking about?" she asks.

"You," Rose and I say together.

"Very funny." Ally looks at me. "What are you waiting for?"

"Nothing." I wrap my hands around the shovel's handle. "You guys ready?" Rose and Ally nod, and I drive the shovel into the ground. After a couple of wimpy spades, I use my foot to push the shovel deeper into the dirt. I scoop up a big mound and toss it aside.

"Go, Birdie. Dig," Ally says, her eyes widening with anticipation.

"Yeah, dig," says Rose with her glass-half-empty tone, but I know she's curious.

So I dig and they remove stray dirt from around the wire. Sweat drips down my face as the hole steadily grows deeper.

"There's nothing down there," Rose says.

"There's something down there all right." I stop digging and wipe my brow.

"Want me to take over?" Ally asks.

I shake my head and start digging again. Another inch. Another six inches. I'm about to give up, when I plunge the shovel down hard.

And *CLUNK*.

Our eyes meet. I've hit something.

Without saying a word, I throw the shovel aside. We start moving dirt with our hands as I grab the wire and see it's connected to something. A handle.

While Rose and Ally scoop away more earth, I pull even harder on the wire. And then, the something down there begins to come up.

"Help me!" I exclaim, and Rose grasps the wire with me while Ally clutches the handle and lifts the thing out of the ground.

A box. Smaller than an average shoe box. Smothered in dirt and clay. Ally places it between us and we just stare, shocked that it's really there.

"What is it?" Ally whispers.

Rose and I don't say anything. Instead I reach out and start cleaning away the stubborn caked dirt while Rose plucks off a leaf from the island bush and starts rubbing the box like it's a genie's lantern. Slowly, and not at all magically, a dull silver surface begins to peek through.

Ally and I grab leaves and help, revealing a silver metal box with a black handle. But there's more. Words. In thick black Magic Marker letters. Across the top of the box is written:

OPEN IF YOU DARE.

"Whoa," I say.

I glance at Ally, who's biting her lip. Rose's eyes are uncharacteristically wide.

"Let's dare," I say and reach to open it.

"Wait!" Rose exclaims.

Ally and I look at her. "Why?"

"What if there *are* bones in there?"

We look at the box, frozen silent.

"There won't be bones," I say.

"Swear?"

I grin. "Swear. Now, come on. Let's do this." I place the box in front of my crossed legs and say, "We three, best friends for life, on our last and best summer together. We dare." I gaze at them one last time. They nod, then I pop the old clasp that holds down the ancient lid.

Carefully, I open the box.

On top rests a single piece of yellowed notebook paper. As I lift it out of the box, our eyes fix on the four words written in bold black letters on the page.

I TOLD YOU SO

I told you so? Who told who what? I look at Ally and Rose. Our eyes meet in a way that says this is serious now. At the bottom of the piece of paper, a black arrow points to the right. I turn the sheet of paper over and see in much smaller writing—normal handwriting, girl's handwriting—a date. June 28, 1973. And a message.

If you're reading this, it says, *I'm already dead.*

2

ALLY IS usually the brave one. She has four older brothers and that's made her tough. But she's the one who inches back while Rose leans forward and whispers, "Go on."

Further down the page, below that ominous line about somebody already being dead, there's more writing. It looks like a poem and I read it out loud.

> *R.D. is not alone anymore.*
> *Because now I'm a dead girl, too.*
> *I could have mailed this (I could have!) but*
> *I'm not going to make it easy for you <u>this</u> time.*
> *You know her address.*
> *Where feathers are hard.*
> *Keep following the clues!*
> *Because he's still out there.*

"Where feathers are hard?" I repeat quietly. "I'm a dead girl, too . . . ?"

"What does that mean?" Ally asks. I look up at Rose and Ally's gaping faces.

"I don't know. It's a clue." My eyes search the box for help. "Look at this."

"Look at what?" Rose asks nervously.

"No bones," I say and reach inside. I pull out a ring—a silver one with an oval black stone on top.

Rose tilts her head, examining it as Ally says, "Looks haunted."

I put it on my ring finger anyway. It fits. And I realize: "This ring—"

"—belonged to a kid," Rose says, finishing my thought. I take it off quickly.

"Somebody like us." Ally shifts forward again. "Let me see." I give her the ring and Ally glides it onto her finger. Holding up her hand, she studies it like it's a precious diamond. "Who would wear a ring like this?"

I'm wondering the same thing, when the black stone turns deep purple right before our eyes.

"Eek!" Ally cries, flinging the ring off like it's a snake coiled around her finger. The ring lands with a *CLINK* back in the box and we watch it magically turn black again.

"It *is* haunted," I say.

"Relax," Rose says, picking it up again. "It's a mood ring."

"What's a mood ring?" I ask.

"A ring that changes colors with your mood." Rose puts it on her finger and we watch it turn blue. "Didn't know they had these back in 1973."

"Yeah, when it belonged to a dead girl," Ally says.

"Good point." Rose says, promptly dropping the ring back into the box again. It lands on a small rectangular card tattooed in black ink.

I pick the card up and hold it to the light. It feels thick between my fingers. "I think it's a ticket."

"A ticket?" Rose reaches out. She takes the ticket and she examines it like it's a relic from a museum. "Allman Brothers Band. The Omni Coliseum," she reads. "From June 2, 1973."

"That was a long time ago," Ally points out.

At the top of the yellowed notebook paper that's resting on my knee, I see the date that's written in girl's handwriting again: *June 28, 1973*. "Look, this note was written in June 1973, too. Less than a month after the...whatever Brothers concert."

"So?" Rose asks.

"So... has this been buried here the whole time?" I feel like I am traveling back in time to 1973. I count back on my fingers. "That's over forty years ago." I don't think my mom was even born yet. "What's that on the back?"

Rose turns over the ticket. "Horrible handwriting. Mrs. Allot would flunk her out of English." She gives it back to me. "You try."

"I think it says Ruth...Ruthie...Dal...Del...Gado."

"Ruthie Delgado?" Ally's face scrunches. "Who's she?"

I look at them, deadly serious. "I think that's what we're supposed to find out."

When I wake up, it's after nine. I smell bacon.

Sliding off the book that's been sleeping on my chest, I slip out of bed. From downstairs, I can already hear Zora. Talking, talking, talking. Walking past my corkboard of selfies, I spy the one Rose took of us in front of the Gillans' house three days ago. It looks like we're smiling except for our eyes. Tiny cracks of uncertainty are now living there, cracks that will surely grow bigger by August.

Our old eyes stare back at me from hundreds of other selfies on the board. Ally, Rose, and me at a violin recital. Us together at a baseball game. Us at the pool. During a field trip. At the local library. There's even one with us and the librarian, Mrs. Thompson.

I head downstairs in my pajamas and lean against the kitchen door. Dad is flipping bacon in the skillet as Zora sits on the counter talking to him. It's the first Monday of summer break, so Mom must have left for work already. The best I can decipher, Zora is recounting a SpongeBob episode, line by line. My dad nods and makes interested noises like he's into it.

"Birdie!" Zora jumps off the counter, runs over, and gives me a hug.

"Morning," Dad says and smiles.

"Morning, Dad."

"Birdie, Birdie, Birdie," Zora says, bouncing up and down. "Look what we got from the basement!" She points at the big chalkboard on wheels that's set up behind the kitchen table. Oh, great.

"I see it." I can hardly contain my excitement.

"We were waiting for you to make Mickey pancakes," Dad says.

"Mickey pancakes!" Zora yells. "Can I help?"

"Sure you can, Ace!" Dad says, and Zora pulls over the step stool as Dad pours batter mix into a big bowl.

I plop into my chair at the kitchen table and stare at the empty chalkboard. Of course Zora is excited. This single chalkboard represents everything that's right and wrong about Zora and our dad.

It's called mathematics.

Don't call it math. Not in our house. My dad is a high school mathematics teacher. He teaches calculus, trigonometry, geometry, and algebra. He knows it all. And loves it all. He thinks it's very important for us to love it, too. So every summer he sets up Super Summer Mathematics Camp.

Zora is the number one participant. It's every day with the two of them. I am required to attend two mornings a week, and since I do it, Rose and Ally sometimes come. It's only for an hour and they like my dad. Or they like me. I don't really know why they do it. I'm just glad when they do.

I am not gifted in mathematics. I would prefer reading a book . . . or solving a puzzle.

My mom is a scientist who likes books but not as much as she likes science. Zora is strangely gifted in both fields. Not sure she can read but she can tell you the square root of three zillion and fourteen without using a calculator. Sometimes I think I was born to the wrong family because I'm so different from them.

"Zora!" I call out. Sheepishly, she looks my way. "What's he doing down here?!"

"You were sleeping and he was lonely."

I roll my eyes and pick up Peg Leg Fred, who is propped up on her chair surrounded by little metal airplanes. Peg Leg Fred is my oldest stuffed animal. He's a polar bear who lost his leg, so Mom and I made him a special bear leg prosthetic, which made Dad call him Peg Leg. "He's not yours."

"I know."

"Come on, Birdie. Loosen up," Dad says as he helps Zora crack an egg over the pancake batter. "In the immortal words of Alice Cooper, 'School's out for summer.'"

"Who's she?" I ask.

Dad shakes his head. "It's a he. And Zora didn't hurt Peg Leg."

I hug Peg Leg to my chest. "Whatever," I whisper but not quietly enough.

"Elizabeth." Dad only calls me Elizabeth when he's not happy with me. My real name is Elizabeth Jade Adams, but Dad started calling me Birdie when I was little.

"Sorry," I say. Our eyes meet. "Really."

He nods. "Okay, then."

Peg Leg sits on my lap while we eat Mickey pancakes. I have three. Zora and I pour more syrup on our bacon than on the pancakes. Dad thinks that's gross. We got that from Mom.

"So, exciting news, girls," Dad says as he eyes the chalkboard. "This summer is going to be all about . . ."

Zora leans forward in anticipation.

"Algebra!" he says.

"Yay!" Zora claps. Her eyes light up as she turns to me. "Birdie, you're going to love it!"

How did I not know my seven-year-old sister was already doing algebra? No wonder she's starting a special school next year.

Dad forks a stack of Mickey ears into his mouth, then continues. "First, we're going to tackle variables, which we sometimes call . . ."

"Vampires!" Zora cries.

"And then from vampires, we'll go to . . ."

I try to concentrate on my pancakes while pasting a smile on my face so I look like I care about the nerd-talk coming out of Dad and Zora. I really do try hard. It's their first day of summer as well, and I know this means a lot to them. I try to look interested. I try to nod at the right places. I try to keep my eyes open but I'm afraid they're glazing over. Because what I'm thinking about is much more important.

The dead girl.

I can't get her out of my head. Ever since we found the box, I've been thinking about Ruthie Delgado and the other girl, the one who wrote the clue and buried the box and might be dead, too. Because as I read and reread the clue all weekend, it's been sinking in what it really means.

Somebody killed Ruthie Delgado. That somebody was a him. And when the other girl went after him, he killed her, too. This is a story of two dead girls. And even though it was a very long time ago, it's up to us to find the next clue so we can solve what happened to them.

"Birdie, you've been staring at your pancakes for five minutes. Did you hear any of that?" My dad's voice pulls me back into our kitchen. Back to our pancake breakfast.

I look up, startled. Because, no, I didn't hear any of that.

He grins at me. "First day of summer gets a pass. Come on. Help me with the dishes."

3

I CAN'T help it. It bothers me that she doesn't answer, that she doesn't wave back.

"Hi, Mrs. Hale," I call out again. But nothing. So why do I keep trying?

After breakfast, I hung out for the first Super Summer Mathematics Camp with Dad and Zora then peeled off for the pool to join Rose and Ally there. Other than Ally's baseball game on Saturday, it's been family time all weekend.

Mrs. Hale lives down the street from us, between my house and the pool. Or between my house and Rose's house. It's practically the same thing. I pass Mrs. Hale's house almost every day in the summer, usually wearing my summer uniform: bathing suit, shorts, and sneakers to protect my feet from the burning asphalt.

Mrs. Hale's house is old and covered in green ivy. There's a brick chimney, a shingled roof, and massive tree limbs hanging overhead. The entire lawn is all bushes and flowers and plants.

Mrs. Hale is digging in her azalea patch, her back turned

to me as I go by. She's wearing jeans and sneakers, her white hair pulled back in a tight old-lady bun.

"Hi." I try one more time, but she keeps pulling up weeds (or something like that) and doesn't acknowledge me in any way. Rose thinks Mrs. Hale must be mean. Ally thinks she's crazy. I'm not exactly sure what I think yet.

Maybe I keep trying because I've lived in this neighborhood my whole life and Mrs. Hale has been here much longer than that. And she lives in that big house all by herself.

Sometimes, when our eyes do meet, she actually gives me a small nod or a little wave, but somehow it feels reluctant. Like she's not so sure about me. And I can't help but wonder . . .

Because my mom is white and my dad is black. Our neighborhood is mostly white and so is my school. I don't think about much about it. Neither do my friends. We're just who we are. Zora and I look alike, a perfect blend of both our parents. Dad calls us his mocha Frappuccinos. Mom calls us the future.

Secretly, I wonder sometimes if Mrs. Hale is one of those old southerners who isn't ready for our kind of future yet.

"Maybe we should go to the police," Ally says.

We're sitting on the side of the pool, feet dangling in the water, our skin quick-drying in the blazing Georgia sun.

"They probably have more important things to do than go chasing after some random clue from some yet to be determined reliable or unreliable source," Rose says.

I eyeball Rose, realizing the curiosity she filled up on

when we discovered the box has been seeping out of her like a slow leak from a three-day-old helium balloon. "You don't know she's not reliable," I say.

"You don't even know she's a she," Rose fires back.

"You saw the handwriting. It was cursive and neat and no boy would write like that."

"Okay," she says, "but how do we know it's for real. It could be a hoax. Some kind of game someone was playing."

"It's not a hoax," I say emphatically. "I think the dead girl—"

"Which one is the dead girl again?" Ally cuts in. "I'm getting confused."

"I think they're both dead!" I say, louder than expected.

"Calm down, love," Rose says, sounding British and a bit superior. I hate it when she does that.

Lowering my voice, I continue. "Okay, listen. Just so we can keep this thing straight, the dead girl is Ruthie Delgado. She was the one who was going to the concert but didn't come back."

"Check," Ally says.

"So what do we call the other girl?" I ask.

"The nutty one," Rose says with a grin, which I reward with my pointy elbow in her arm.

"How about the Girl Who Buried the Box?" offers Ally.

"Groan," says Rose. "I'm not saying that mouthful every time."

"Yeah," I say. "We need a *name*."

"Like what?" Ally asks.

"I don't know." So I think. This girl was trying to solve a

mystery. She was on the trail of a murderer. What do you call somebody like that? "Girl Detective!" I suddenly blurt out. "You know, like Nancy Drew?"

"Who?" Rose asks.

"Nancy Drew, comma, Girl Detective. Don't you ever read?"

"Not since the Internet was invented," Rose says. Taken literally, that means she's never read a book in her entire life.

"You've seen them on my shelves. The Nancy Drew mysteries. It's a series. Like Harry Potter but a ton more." I'm met with blank stares. "My mom gave me her books from when she was our age. Nancy Drew's a teenager who solved mysteries long before our Girl Detective came along."

"Oh, you mean like Sherlock Holmes?" Rose asks.

"Exactly like him, except for the hundred ways that they're different."

"I like calling her Girl Detective," Ally says. "Makes her sound official."

Rose nods. "I could go with that."

"Yeah, me too. Girl Detective it is."

"Great!" Ally says, kicking her legs and making a splash. "Now we can go to the police."

"I think that was the whole point of the clue," I say.

Ally looks at me. "What do you mean?"

Since the box has been hiding under my bed all weekend, I've had plenty of time to memorize the clue. "Because Girl Detective said, and I quote, *I could have mailed this (I could have!) but I'm not going to make it easy for you this time.* Which means to me that she told someone official and they didn't listen to her."

"How do you know she told someone official?" Ally asks.

"I don't for sure, but if I were Girl Detective, it's what I would have done."

"You would have told the police?" Rose asks, like she doesn't believe me.

"Yes, I would have. And I think she told the police. But they didn't listen."

"Even if she did, that was the 1970s police," Ally says. "Police would pay attention now."

That's not exactly what my dad would say but maybe she's right. "But if we tell the police—"

"—the police will tell our parents," Rose continues. "Could you imagine what my mom would say?"

"So let's just tell *a* parent," Ally says.

"The General?" I ask.

"Well . . . ," says Ally. We call Ally's mom the General. Not to her face or anything. Just to ourselves. Mrs. Lorenz (the General) runs their household like a military commander. She works all week as a paralegal secretary downtown, so the kids have to fend for themselves a lot and really help out at home. "Maybe not her. I was thinking more about your dad."

"If we tell my dad, he'll want to know where we found the clue. And the box," I say. "And then we'll be busted about the island." My parents trust me. And mostly they don't worry about us as long as we stick together. But there are certain rules. Like: *Stay in the neighborhood. Don't go past the pool.* If we told them about the island, we'd be banned from there forever.

Ally sighs. "So . . ."

"Yeah, so," echoes Rose.

A whistle blows, and my eyes turn to the lifeguard chair elevated between the regular pool and the deep end. Mrs. Franklin has been our lifeguard for as long as I can remember and she runs the pool area like the General runs Ally's family. Even though she's sheltered under a big sun umbrella, her white skin is already on its way to leather brown. A familiar dab of zinc oxide streaks the bridge across her nose.

"I tried to google Ruthie Delgado," I say. "To find out where she lived and stuff."

"And?" asks Rose.

"Nothing. Couldn't find anything. Like she's a ghost or something."

"A dead ghost," Ally says gravely.

"I found the Allman Brothers, though."

"Yeah?" says Rose.

"Yeah. They were a rock band. From Jacksonville, Florida. Gregg and . . ." I struggle to remember the other one's name. "Duane, I think. Yeah, that's it. Duane Allman. The band moved here—"

Ally brightens. "To Georgia?"

I nod. "They had super-long man hair and weird mustaches. I'll show you the pictures. One of them died in a motorcycle accident, though."

"Which one?" Ally asks.

"I don't remember." And I feel bad about that. It feels like an insult to either Gregg or Duane so I try to remember harder. "Duane, I think."

"Before or after Ruthie went to their concert?" Rose asks.

"Pretty sure before," I say uncertainly. "So she must have just seen Gregg."

"So somebody went to a rock concert," Rose says. "A hundred years ago."

"That somebody was Ruthie Delgado. *She* went to a rock concert," I say. "It's got to mean something. Or Girl Detective wouldn't have put a ticket with Ruthie's name on it in the box."

"Maybe it means our one-eyed pirate buried some random ticket instead of some animal bones."

"Big help, Rose," I say. "Thanks a lot."

"Maybe they've been dead so long that nobody would care anyway," Ally says. I can tell she's not thinking about Ruthie or Girl Detective. She's thinking about her father.

When Ally was two, her dad died of a heart attack while he was taking his morning run. Her brothers remember their dad, but Ally doesn't and that really bothers her. Her dad was a huge baseball fan. When Ally was a baby, they were at an Atlanta Braves game and her dad caught a home run while holding Ally in his arms. It was on the news and everything. Ally has seen the video so many times she's convinced herself that she remembers it. But how could she?

"Somebody cares," I say. "Somebody always cares."

4

ALLY IS in a slump.

"What is happening out there?" the General says quietly. Rose and I sit beside Ally's mom in the bleachers. We, along with everyone else in the stands, are watching in disbelief as Ally walks the third batter in a row. Her team, the Hunters, is already behind by two runs.

Rose leans into me. "This is bad. Like last week all over again."

Ally's coach calls time-out and walks to the mound. Last Saturday, we sat in this same spot and watched Ally pitch the worst game of her life. It was shocking because that's never happened to her before. Ally always pitches great.

We hardly talked about it afterward. I think we were hoping whatever was wrong would magically fix itself.

It hasn't.

"She can't be great every week," Mark says from the other side of Ally's mom. Mark is the youngest of Ally's older brothers and the one who taught her to play baseball.

The General shoots him a look that says *No talking trash*

about your sister, but Mark just shrugs. "I'm going to get a Coke," he says and jumps down from the bleachers.

Mark is two years older than Ally. When Ally was in second grade, Mark gave her his old glove and started throwing with her. In the years since, she's become better at baseball than him—and practically everyone else. This year he decided not to play anymore. Says he's gotten too old for Little League.

"Girls, do you know what's going on with Ally?" her mom asks as we watch Ally walk, eyes low, back to the dugout. The replacement pitcher, Charles Johnson, takes the mound.

"No," I say.

"No idea," says Rose.

"Well, there's something wrong," she says.

Ally takes a seat in the dugout with the second- and third-string players. She doesn't belong there. I realize the General is right. Something *is* wrong with Ally. But what?

After the game, we sit under the tree down from the third base dugout and eat snow cones while the next teams take the field. Ally's white baseball pants are streaked with dirt. She throws down her cap and pulls the ponytail holder out of her long blond hair like it's her mortal enemy.

The General and Mark have left already. Ally's house isn't far from the ball field, so we'll walk there after our snow cones.

"It'll be better next week," I say, trying to cheer her up.

Ally groans and throws her head back.

"Don't listen to her, Al," Rose says. "It'll suck next week, too. Don't worry about it."

Ally throws her cap at Rose, almost toppling her snow cone.

"Kidding!" Rose exclaims. "Geez, Al."

"What did Mark say?" Ally asks.

"I don't know. I don't think he said anything." I look at Rose. "Did he say anything?"

Rose shrugs. "What would he have to say?"

"I don't know," says Ally. "Oh, crap."

We follow Ally's gaze and see Joey Wachowski walking our way, flanked by Connor and Romeo. Their baseball gloves are tucked under their arms and a bat is slung over Joey's shoulder. They all wear blue baseball shirts sporting their team's name, the Broncos. "Hope they lost," Ally utters quietly.

Joey looks up at the scoreboard hanging over left field. Orioles 6, Hunters 1. "Too bad, Lorenz! What's it like to be the worst girl pitcher in the league? Oh, I mean the only girl pitcher in the league. Or is it the same thing?" He laughs. "Your championship dreams are slipping away, Blondie."

"Shut up, Joey," Ally says.

"Why don't you make me?" Joey shoots back.

"I'll make you," Romeo says and punches Joey in the shoulder. Not hard. But hard enough.

"I'll kick your butt, Rome," Joey threatens. But Romeo is not threatened. He just smiles.

"Hi, Romeo." Rose's flirty voice calls out from beside me.

"Hi." He looks down at us, the sun haloing his head. "Y'all coming to the pool later?" Connor lives in our neighborhood, and Romeo and Joey come over a lot.

"Maybe," Rose says.

Romeo looks at me.

"No, we're going to Ally's," I say quickly. "Her mom is expecting us."

"We don't have to go," Rose says.

"Yes, we do." I look at Ally, then nudge Rose's arm.

"Yeah, we gotta go," Rose says back. "She needs a Red Vine infusion."

"We won, by the way. On a streak," Joey says. "Pitched a no-hitter." He pops his gum dramatically. "Way things are going, we might not meet again, Blondie."

I'll translate: All the teams have one more game in the regular season. Then the championship playoffs begin. The way the championship brackets are set up, the Hunters and the Broncos will play again only if they meet in the final championship game. And whoever wins the championship game plays the winner of the Dunwoody league in the big charity game in August.

Joey goes on. "Hate to break it to you, Blondie, but if you can't lead your team to a Little League championship, there's no chance of you making it on the middle school team!"

Now he's gone too far. Ally's about to serve up a rude hand gesture, when Rose says, "She'll be in the championships."

Everyone looks at Rose.

"In fact, the Hunters are going to win. You watch, Joey." Oh yeah. That's how she does it. Cool Rose has a big mouth when it comes to sticking up for her friends.

"Right." Joey laughs. "How much you wanna bet?"

"How much *you* wanna bet?" she says.

"Against the Broncos! That's crazy!"

"Don't call me crazy!" Rose springs to her feet and squares off in front of Joey, which looks pretty hilarious because Joey is practically twice the size of her in every direction. "A hundred bucks!" she says. "A hundred bucks that Ally beats you!"

"No money," Romeo says.

"Yeah, no money," I say and nod to Romeo.

"Then what?" Connor asks.

"It's got to be good," barks Joey.

"It'll be good," Rose says and starts pacing in a circle, starting to think.

"How about this?" Romeo says, and Rose stops. "What if . . . the loser has to ride in the Fourth of July parade wearing the winning team's jersey?"

"That's not bad," I say. Every Fourth of July, there's a big parade in our neighborhood. There are floats and people riding in convertibles and everything. It would be fun to see Joey waving to the crowd in a Hunters shirt while getting soaked by water cannons from the crowd.

"Yeah." Rose eyes Romeo. "I like it."

"Okay," Joey says. He spits in the palm of his hand and holds it out.

"Gross!" Rose says. "I'm not shaking that!"

"No shake, no bet."

Rose's head rolls back. "Fine, then. It's a bet." She hesitates, then sticks out her hand. They shake and Joey holds on a little too long. "Give me back my hand, you disgusting slob." He does and Rose can't wipe off her infected palm soon enough.

"Cool," says Joey. He looks down at Ally, who's been strangely silent while Rose was betting her life away. "See ya, suckers!" Smiling and waving his bat around, Joey takes off toward the concession stand, Connor by his side.

Romeo rolls his eyes. "Sorry, Ally." Then he smiles at us. "Later."

Once they're out of earshot, Ally looks up. "Thanks a lot. I can't wait to be in the parade."

"We've got two weeks before the play-offs start to figure this thing out," I say.

"You can't be in a slump forever," adds Rose. "It'll be okay."

"Yeah, right. You saw me out there today."

"Yeah," I tell her. "We saw."

"If Joey wins the championship, he's going to make the middle school team. He'll be the sixth-grade pitcher, and I'll be nothing. You know that, right?"

Rose and I swap glances. Ally and Joey will be going to the old middle school together in August. There's only one spot for a sixth-grade pitcher on the team.

Ally turns and looks over at Joey. "I hate that guy."

"I like that guy," Rose says, and we both glare at her. "Romeo!" She says defensively.

"Cut it out, Rose," I say and turn toward the concession stand. I find myself looking at Romeo and see he's looking at me, too.

5

FOURTEEN RED Vines in, and Ally and Rose are laughing, but not me. We're hanging out in Ally's kitchen trying to come up with a play-off plan, but every time we get serious, Trixie farts. Trixie is Ally's golden retriever. She's old and can't help it. Usually, I would join in. (In the laughing, not the farting.)

When Ally gets up to grab more popcorn, Rose leans in. "What's with the serious, Bird? Ally's going to be okay."

Rose thinks I'm thinking about Ally. I'm not. "Oh, I know," I hear myself saying. First lie. "I was just thinking about the clue." Second lie. "Remember when it said: *Where feathers are hard*? What do you think Girl Detective was talking about?"

"Why are you so obsessed with this?" She draws a long breath. "I don't know. It doesn't make sense because feathers can't be hard."

"Yeah, that's what I was thinking." Third lie.

"Can we just focus on Ally?"

"Yeah. Sure." But I can't focus on Ally because I can't

stop thinking about Rose. The serious Rose saw on my face wasn't about Ally and it wasn't about the clue. It was about her. Rose. And what she'll think if she ever finds out.

It started on Valentine's Day. Rose was expecting a Valentine's card from Romeo. She had decided to like him, and usually Rose gets what Rose wants. On Valentine's Day, our fifth grade class was decorated in hearts and BE MINE cutouts. Along the back shelf, everyone had a bag with their name on it, also decorated in hearts and dorky cutouts, and throughout the day we all put candy or cards into one another's bags. It's a rule that you have to bring something for everyone. Rose was surprised that she didn't get something special from Romeo. She decided he must be shy.

Romeo is not shy. After school, when I was going through my V-Day loot at the kitchen table, I found an envelope at the very bottom of the bag, my name written on it in delicate red ink. It was during the hour before Dad got home from work, so it was just me and Zora. While she was watching TV, I walked the envelope upstairs and closed my bedroom door behind me.

I looked at the writing for a long time. I imagined a secret fairy had singled me out or a Valentine genie had written to grant me a special Valentine's wish. Because no kid in my class had handwriting as neat and nice as that! I was enjoying the mystery until I heard Zora yelling for me. The envelope went under my pillow and for the rest of the afternoon, I made up scenarios about its imaginary source.

When I finally opened it before going to bed, I had to read it again and again.

Dear Birdie,
Roses are red
Violets are blue
Didn't want a girlfriend
Until I met you.

Forever yours . . .

And then a signature.

Romeo's signature.

Romeo D., he'd signed it.

Girlfriend? Romeo? What?! I wasn't ready to be some-body's girlfriend! And lots of girls liked Romeo. Rose liked Romeo! What was he thinking?

I didn't show it to anyone. Not even my mom. I hid it in one of my favorite books, *When You Reach Me,* and put it back on the shelf. Nobody I know would look there.

"Earth to Bird."

"Huh?"

"Quit thinking about the clue already. We've got to go," Rose says and gets up from Ally's table, which is still covered with Red Vines. "Violin."

"Yeah," I say. "Hey, is your brother home?"

"Probably," answers Rose.

I look at Ally. "Maybe he can help us."

"If you're pitching like that, we could use you on the high school team," Simon says after Ally throws another perfect pitch into his glove.

"I'm not pitching like that, though," she says.

Simon looks at me. "She's really not pitching like that," I say. I've been sitting on the porch of Rose's house watching them for at least half an hour, while the sound of Rose's violin wafts into the front yard. It's a very sad song she's practicing today. Over and over again. As my eyes fall upon the FOR SALE sign on their front yard, I feel a tiny hook tug at the bottom of my heart.

"Hmm." Simon thinks and throws the baseball back to Ally. "It must be psychological, then." Simon is the first-string catcher of the high school team. He knows all about pitchers and slumps. If anyone can help Ally, Simon can.

"Psychological?" Ally says. "What does that mean?"

Simon stands from his catcher's squat and walks to her. "Pitching is not just about being able to throw a ball," he says. "There's a lot more to it. Mentally, I mean. You see it all the time. Pitchers get in a slump because of lots of things. They let the pressure get to them. Or somebody says something bad about them. Or they lose a game and can't recover. Happens all the time. The main question is: What's different about pitching in the front yard versus pitching in the game?"

"I don't know," Ally says. "I've never had a problem before."

This is true. Ally pitches like a machine. At least she used to. That's why her teammates love her and why Joey Wachowski pretends she's no good.

Rose's mom appears through the screen at the front door. "Simon, Ashley's on the phone. Said she couldn't reach you on your mobile."

Simon pats his pocket for his cell phone that's clearly not there. "Oh yeah." He looks back at Ally as he steps onto the front porch. "So think about it, okay? It's got to be about something."

As he slips through the screen door past his mom, she rolls her eyes at us. "Girlfriends," she utters so only we can hear. Rose's mom has dark hair like Rose and the same blue eyes. As she retreats back inside, Ally sits down beside me on the stairs.

"He thinks I have a mental problem," she says.

"We know you have a mental problem," I say, then grin. "Simon just thinks you have an additional one."

"Hilarious, Birdie."

"You think it's a boob problem?" I ask.

"No!" she says a little too quickly.

"Sorry. Just asking." Ally's younger than me and Rose, but she's definitely older in the boob department.

"I've got on a bra *and* an ACE bandage," she says. "I'm pushing them down as much as I can. I was pitching great three weeks ago. And they're not any bigger now than they were then." She looks down at her chest just to be sure. "At least I hope not."

"Then what is it? What's wrong?"

She shrugs.

"A boy?"

"Right." Ally punches my shoulder. I don't think Ally knows how pretty she is. I bet some boys will be noticing soon.

"We've got to beat the Broncos," she says. "If we don't, Joey will pitch the charity game. It will probably be against the Condors again. And if he wins that, they'll pick him for the middle school team." She sighs, then points to her chest. "I can't let these or anything else get in my way."

6

IF YOU'RE *reading this, I'm already dead.* Rose is right. I am obsessed.

The box is open on my bed. Once again I'm staring at Girl Detective's handwriting, rereading the cryptic clue.

Who was Ruthie Delgado? How did she die? And who was Girl Detective? She must have had a name and a reason for burying the box and writing the clue.

Gazing at the Nancy Drew mysteries on my shelf, I wonder if Nancy ever had to solve *two* murders.

Rose, Ally, and I were at the pool all morning before I came back home to eat some lunch and pick up Zora. I was supposed to be on Zora duty for the afternoon and was planning to work on her swim strokes. I'm a very good swimmer—was on the swim team for three years—but Zora is not a duck who takes to water. She's timid in the pool and I want to help her be brave.

On my way home, I passed Mrs. Hale's house. I stopped and listened to the breeze whispering through her creepy trees. Mrs. Hale was nowhere to be seen but I gave her a little wave anyway. She's in that big house so covered with ivy it might eat her alive. I imagine her waving back at me from behind her curtains.

As I cut through our next door neighbors' Japanese gardens, I saw Mom's car parked in our driveway. Something was up. She was supposed to be at work.

Mom is a research scientist at the CDC. That's the Center for Disease Control. She studies weird diseases and stuff like that. Science-y stuff. Stuff I don't really care about and stuff that scares me sometimes.

"Mom!" I yelled as I came in.

"In the kitchen, Birdie."

"What are you doing here?" I asked, stopping cold when I saw the multiple jars of mayonnaise, ketchup, mustard, jam, olives, horseradish, and other assorted hundred-year-old condiments laid out on our kitchen table.

"I live here," she said.

"Very funny."

She twisted off the lid of a mayo jar, took a sniff, and pulled a sour face. "Oh, that has got to go," she said, placing the jar on the counter before looking back at me. "Hey, baby."

"What are you doing, Mom?"

"Zora doesn't feel well and she wanted me to come home."

"What's wrong with her?"

"My professional opinion?" She lowered her voice. "I think she needs some mama love . . . and your dad could use a day to himself."

"So why are you cleaning out the refrigerator?"

"Because I've discovered it's not so much a refrigerator as

a petri dish. You can't imagine some of the bacteria that's been growing in there."

With Mom it always comes back to science. "Comforting to know," I said, plopping down at the table. "Dad usually makes us lunch about now."

"I can make lunch. Look at these olives," she said with horrified delight as she held out the jar to me. I practically puked. "It's fascinating what's at the back of the fridge."

"That's so gross."

"It's all a matter of perspective. What kind of sandwich would you like? I was thinking—"

"No peanut butter and banana," I said firmly.

"Oh," she said, puzzled. "Then what?" She looked inside the open refrigerator door and pulled out a plastic bag of meat. "Turkey looks good."

"Yes, please!"

As Mom stood at the counter making the sandwiches, I grouped the jars and bottles as neatly as possible to the far side of table.

"Penny for your thoughts?" she asked while dealing turkey slices onto three pieces of bread.

"A penny isn't much."

"Guess it hasn't been adjusted for inflation since your nana used to say it to me. What should it be?"

"Ten dollars?" I said, hopefully.

"Dream on, kid. I wasn't born yesterday."

"When *were* you born? What year, I mean?"

"Way back in 1975."

"What was it like back then?" I asked.

"I don't know. I was a baby."

"I bet Aunt Lisa knows."

"Yes, because Aunt Lisa is much older than me and she remembers everything." She brought two plates of turkey sandwiches, potato chips, and pickles and placed one in front of me.

I examined the pickle. "Is this safe to eat?"

"I'm a scientist. You can trust me." She took a huge bite out of her pickle.

I felt a sudden urge to tell her everything. About the box. About the ticket. About the Allman Brothers Band. But instead I asked, "Could you and Dad have been married if we lived back then?"

"When?"

"The 1970s."

Mom paused. Whenever I bring up race stuff, she always gets really thoughtful. Unlike Dad, who will say practically anything.

"Not impossible. But I think it would have been hard. Especially someplace like here." She meant Atlanta. The South. My mom grew up in Atlanta but my dad's from Chicago.

"Is it hard now?"

"No. Mostly. But there are moments," she said, raising an eyebrow. "You've seen how it can be sometimes."

I thought back to that time in the grocery store when an older white lady complimented Mom on her beautiful daughter, Ally. When my mom corrected her and told her that I was the daughter, the woman huffed and walked away.

"But it doesn't happen often," Mom said. "Thankfully, the world is always changing."

I nodded and took a bite of my sandwich.

"You've never asked me that before," she said with a smile. "My girl is getting all grown up."

"Birdie?"

I turned to see Zora standing at the door to the kitchen, thumb in mouth, and holding a miniature rocket in her other hand. Her knees were peeking through the holes of her Doc McStuffins pajamas and her soft 'fro was in tangles.

"Zora, we've gotta do your hair," I said.

"I did her hair," Mom said as Zora curled up in her lap like a three-year-old.

I smiled at my blond-haired, blue-eyed mom. She tries, but she's terrible at black hair. I remember walking around in a matted mess until my dad's mom taught me how to do it right. Then I finally got my braids and life became so much easier.

"Zora needs braids, Mom," I said, partly because I'm tired of doing it and partly because Zora needs all the help she can get. "Professional ones."

"Can we wait until she's eight to talk about that? Can't I keep one of my girls little for at least one more summer?"

"Do I have fever, Mommy?" Zora asked pitifully.

Mom felt her forehead. "No, sweetheart. No fever." She kissed Zora on the cheek. "I know. Why don't we play a game?"

"Mom, they're waiting for me at the pool!" If Zora was sick, I could just hang out with my friends. We could even sneak away to the island for the afternoon.

"It's just one day, Birdie," Mom said. "Why don't you stay home with us?"

I stared at them, Mom and Zora, and thought: *What do you do when your mom's home from work and your sister's sick and your friends are at the pool and the great mystery of your life's waiting for you in a box under your bed?*

You play Candy Land.

For a dumb kid's board game, it took longer than you'd think. Especially because we played it twice. After that, we baked chocolate chip cookies and sang to Zora's favorite music. Finally, I texted Rose from Mom's phone that I wouldn't be back for the day, blaming it on sick Zora.

Once Zora curled up in front of a movie, I slipped upstairs and pulled the clue box out from under my bed. The bright day had turned ominous gray. I studied the clouds through the window. Cumulus coming in from the west (thanks, Science Mom). A gong of thunder threatened in the distance and rolled in like a surfer on a wave.

Cross-legged on my bed, I read the words again. For the hundredth time, I put on my Nancy Drew hat and concentrate on the clue, line by line.

If you're reading this, I'm already dead. Okay, that's pretty clear. Girl Detective buried the box before she was . . . dead. But who was supposed to be reading this?

Not me. We found it by accident. It must have been meant for somebody else. Somebody in 1973. Maybe an official somebody. But who? And why didn't they find it back then?

R.D. is not alone anymore. That's easy. R.D. is Ruthie Delgado. R.D. must have died. Or was murdered. But how?

And what does the ticket have to do with it? And what about the mood ring that Ally thinks is haunted?

Because now I'm a dead girl, too. Even though this happened long ago, it's hard to read this. Especially by myself, alone in my room. Girl Detective buried the box and left the clues. She once wore the ring and held the ticket in her hand. Why does she have to be dead, too?

I could have mailed this (I could have!) but . . . Well, that would have made it a lot easier, for sure. And much more efficient for whoever was supposed to read this in 1973.

I'm not going to make it easy for you this time. Couldn't be less easy, but I can't shake this feeling that she did tell someone. She solved the crime of Ruthie Delgado, told an adult (maybe the police), and they didn't believe her. After all, she wrote the words *I TOLD YOU SO.* And what happens on every TV show when nobody believes you? You go after the killer yourself!

You know her address. Whose address? Ruthie's? I've looked for it online—I'm guessing she lived in the neighborhood, maybe?—but there's no trace of her or her family. It's like all the Delgados simply vanished.

Where feathers are hard. I still have no idea what that means. Little help, G.D.?

Keep following the clues! Okay, but we only have two. A ring and a ticket. But where are they taking us?

Because he's still out there. Even though this clue was written in 1973, and he might not be out there anymore, I feel a shiver run through my body. Who is he? Who *was* he? And what did he do to Ruth Delgado?

I turn over the yellowed notepaper and stare at the words *I TOLD YOU SO* again. Yeah, she must have told somebody and they didn't believe her. And our Girl Detective was mad, I just know it. Really angry that nobody listened. I'm a little angry for her now.

I'm about to flip the piece of paper back over when I see it. On the bottom right-hand corner of the page. Little ink marks. I've noticed them before but they were so small, I didn't think anything of them. Just some inky scratches. But . . .

Hopping off the bed, I reach into my desk drawer and extract my magnifying glass. I hold it steady over the corner of the page. Squinting through the glass, I pull the image into focus.

It's a tiny stick figure. Crudely drawn but unmistakable. A drawing of a little bird.

PART 2

A BIRD IN PLAIN SIGHT

7

"BUT WHAT do you think it means?" I say, pointing at the inky bird at the bottom of the yellowed page.

Ally studies it through my magnifying glass. "You sure it's a bird?"

"Looks like a bird to me."

"Let me see." Rose grabs the glass and looks, too. "Could be."

"It's definitely a bird!" I exclaim.

We're sitting on the island, much like we did the day we found the clue except today Rose is leaning against our willow. It's strangely cool, gray clouds threatening overhead.

Rose hands me back the magnifying glass. "So it's a bird. Are we any closer to understanding any of it?"

"Well, I'm sure she told someone," I say. "Or else, why would she have written *I TOLD YOU SO* like that?" I point to the words as if entering courtroom evidence.

"Have you ever thought that the person she told—"

I cut in. "Maybe the police."

"Maybe the police," she says, "determined that Girl

Detective was not so reliable. Or as I would say, probably cuckoo."

"Why do you have to be that way about Girl Detective?" I say. "What did she ever do to you?"

"I don't know," Rose says. "Maybe it's because it's our last summer together and it feels like there are four girls on this island instead of three."

Ally's eyes meet mine. "It is our last summer together."

I feel myself deflating. I know it's our last summer together. I know we should just be having fun. But I can't seem to help feeling like Girl Detective is real and somehow calling out to me.

"On a happier note," Rose says with a sarcastic edge, "my parents have announced our move date. August 14."

"That's less than two months away!" I exclaim.

"Do you think it was always their evil plan to move me all the way across the ocean, bide their time, and then, when I'm practically American, rip me right back out again?"

"It's so unfair," Ally says, and I know she's saying it for all of us. The unfairness of being separated. None of us ever asked for that.

"You know how traumatic it was when I first came," Rose continues. "I didn't know anybody. I was dressed funny—"

"Really funny," Ally says innocently. But that's not how Rose takes it.

"That's what they wore in England, Al! I couldn't help it!"

I remember. It was the middle of the year in Ms. Hillbrook's first grade class. Ally sat in the desk beside me but we weren't friends yet. When Principal Smith walked through the door with this little skinny girl with jet-black hair and enormous blue eyes, everybody stared at her. Even me. She was wearing a uniform that made me wonder if her last school had been Hogwarts.

Principal Smith cleared her throat and announced, "Class, I'd like to introduce to you a new student, all the way from the United Kingdom."

Bethany Hopkins raised her hand from the second row and talked before being called on. "She's from a kingdom? Like a princess or something?"

Everybody laughed and I saw small pink blotches sprout on the girl's pale white face.

"No," Principal Smith said. "This is India Ashcroft. She's from England, which is part of the United Kingdom, which includes the countries of England, Scotland, Wales, and Northern Ireland."

The girl pulled on Principal Smith's sleeve. "What is it, India?" she asked, leaning down to listen. "Oh," Principal Smith said. "I apologize." She turned to us. "This is Rose. She goes by Rose." She looked down and Rose nodded. I will forever think of this as Rose's first act of independence in the New World.

"Remember, she called you India?" I say to Rose as a breeze ripples through the willow tree branches. I found out later that Rose was her middle name.

"Yeah, I remember." She wraps her arms around her knees. "They better not think they can call me that again when we're back in England. Because they can't. I am not a country! I am a human being!"

A rumble of thunder, like a brooding kettledrum, vibrates through the sky. Instantly, Rose jumps to her feet. We linger and Rose's hands go to her hips. I don't think it's the moment to tell her she looks just like her mother when she does that. "Come on. Let's buzz," she says. "What are you waiting for?"

Rose is no longer that timid girl from first grade. She is fearless and bold and nobody gives her grief. Not anymore. By second grade she had buried her English accent so completely that no one ever guessed she was British. Not only did she blend in, she became the most popular girl in school.

That's why it's always a surprise to me when she's so afraid of rain and thunder.

We follow Rose back to her house under gray clouds so swollen with raindrops they look like they hurt.

"Cuppa tea, girls?" Mrs. Ashcroft calls out from the kitchen as she hears us bolt through the front door. "Rain's coming." What I've learned from Rose's mom is that every event—bad or good—is made better somehow by a cup of tea.

"No thanks, Mum," Rose says. "Going up." That's how you can tell that Rose is actually British underneath it all. Because she calls her mom Mum. As we follow her up the stairs, my eyes glimpse the living room. The moving boxes are multiplying like jackrabbits in there.

As soon as we close Rose's bedroom door, she says, "I want to show you something."

Ally plops down on one of Rose's twin beds and I stretch out on the other one.

"I wonder what Romeo's doing right now," Rose calls out from inside her closet.

"I hope he's beating the crap out of Joey at cards or something," says Ally.

Rose reappears holding a bathing suit up against her clothes. "What do you think?"

"It's a two-piece." My mouth falls open slightly because there's so little bathing suit there.

"It's a bikini!" Rose says. "Nobody calls it a two-piece, Bird."

"I do. Your mom's going to let you wear that?"

"She said."

"My mom would stroke out," Ally deadpans from the bed.

I grin. Because her mom would stroke out. Even Joey's eyeballs would pop out of his head if he saw Ally in something like that.

Then I realize why the tiny bikini is okay with Rose's mother. Because in some ways, Rose still looks like a nine-year-old girl. She used to joke, *I'm light as a feather, flat as a board*. She doesn't say that anymore.

I fold my arms across my chest. Things are starting to change for me under there, but I haven't told them yet. My mom is pretty flat-chested, but I don't take after her. I know that already. I'm like my dad's mom, my grandma—short waist, long legs, and other stuff I don't have yet. Stuff that tells me if I were on a highway, I'd be approaching a sign that reads CURVES AHEAD.

"Do you think he'll like it?" Rose asks as she models in front of the mirror.

"God, I hope not!" Ally beans her with a pillow.

"Al!" Rose yells and throws it back. She places the bikini

on a chair and sits down on the foot of Ally's bed. "If I weren't moving," she says thoughtfully, "I think Romeo would be asking me to the sixth-grade dance."

A knot of guilt twists in my stomach.

The sixth-grade dance is in September at the new middle school where Romeo and I will be going. It's where Rose would be going if she weren't moving away.

"It's not a real dance," I say. "It's after school. You're not supposed to have a date or anything."

"It would have been a real dance for us," Rose says dreamily.

"Let's listen to music," I say, trying to change the subject.

"Okay." Rose goes to her computer. "What do you want to listen to?"

"Don't care," Ally says.

"Something good." I lean back against the pillow and for the first time, I almost feel glad that Rose is moving. Because I know Romeo's not going to ask her to the dance. And that would be horrible to watch. Then I'm struck with a panicky thought: *What if he asks me?!*

"Check this out," Rose says, and the music starts. It's a weird rock song. Twangy, almost country. Something Rose would never play.

Ally and I prop up on our elbows and look at Rose with questioning eyes.

She smiles. "The Allman Brothers Band."

8

"**DO YOU** like the Allman Brothers Band?" I ask my parents at dinner that night.

"The Allman Brothers?" my dad asks, shaking his head and scooping more mashed potatoes onto his plate.

"What's wrong with the Allman Brothers?" Mom says. "I like them okay."

Dad shrugs. "Nothing, I guess."

"Snob," she says. "Zora, eat." Zora's playing with her planes instead of eating her dinner, and the rain is pelting so hard against the kitchen window it almost looks like someone's spraying it with a garden hose.

"Better put out some candles," Dad says. "Just in case."

"We gonna lose 'lectricity?" Zora asks.

"Might," says Dad. He looks up at the ceiling as if he can see through to the sky.

"Why do you ask?" Mom says. "About the Allman Brothers?"

Other than what I've read online, I still don't know much about the Allman Brothers. When Rose played us one of their weird songs, it only left me wanting to know more. So I decide to take a risk. I pull the concert ticket out of my back pocket and place it on the table. My mom stares at it like it's a ticket to Mars. "Rex, look at this," she says to my dad. "Where'd you get this, Birdie?"

"That's not material," I say. That's what lawyers say in a courtroom when they don't want to answer the question. Smart, right?

"Not material?" asks Mom.

"Correct. Not material."

She shakes her head. "All right, Perry Mason."

"Who's she?" I ask.

"He!" my parents answer in unison.

"Okay, okay. Rose found it." Rose would call this a Greater-Good lie. The real and whole truth would expose everything, and I don't think that would serve the greater good at this time. At least not my greater good. I continue. "My question is—what's interesting or . . . revealing about this ticket?"

My mom examines it closely. "It's old."

Dad leans in. "It's strange it wasn't used."

What?! I pick up the ticket. What did I miss? "How do you know she didn't use it?"

"Because the whole ticket's there." My dad says it slowly like he's speaking to a five-year-old or an alien from another planet.

I don't understand. My parents grin at each other. "Explain, please!"

"See that perforation down the middle?" Dad says. "Those little dots are where you can pull it apart."

I look down at the ticket. "Yeah . . . ?"

"When we went to concerts, back in the Stone Age, the man at the door would rip the ticket in half," Dad says. "Right along that perforated line."

"He'd keep half and give you the other half," Mom adds. "And your half was called . . . wait for it . . ."

". . . a ticket stub," they say together, like it's the secret to the universe. They are so dorky sometimes.

"My sister had ticket stubs taped all over her mirror in her bedroom," Mom says. "Lisa went to lots of concerts."

"I bet she did," Dad says.

They keep joking about Mom's older sister but I'm not listening anymore. I'm looking at the ticket and realizing that Ruthie Delgado never used it. She never went to the concert.

But why?

Our local library is less than ten minutes from my house. I've been coming here my whole life. Standing at the checkout counter, I wait for Mrs. Thompson, the librarian, and can't help but read the new poster up on the wall behind the counter.

COME MEET BESTSELLING AUTHOR AND ATLANTA NATIVE

EMILY McALLISTER

SIGNING HER NEW MYSTERY NOVEL

I DON'T KNOW WHY SHE SWALLOWED THE FLY

AUGUST 12 AT NOON

In the photo on the poster is Emily McAllister. She's a white woman with short reddish-blond hair and round black-rimmed glasses, older than my parents (maybe Aunt Lisa's age), and the kind of person my mom would call quirky.

"I just put that up," Mrs. Thompson says as she steps out of the back room, closing the door behind her. "Should be quite the event. You and your dad should come."

"That'd be fun. I've never been to a real live book signing with a real live author before."

"It *is* fun," she says and scans a book into the computer. "How's your summer going, Birdie?"

Hmm. I wonder what she would think if I actually told her. "Fine. Dad and Zora are picking out books."

It thunders outside and she peeks out at the stormy afternoon. "Good day for it."

"I was wondering." I lean onto the counter. "Do you keep any old yearbooks here from any of the local schools? From maybe the 1970s?" I look up at her hopefully.

"That's a strange question," Mrs. Thompson answers. "There are many treasures in this library, but none of the yearbook variety. Why do you ask?"

"No reason."

She cocks her head questioningly, so I change the subject. "Or do you have anything new I should know about?"

Mrs. Thompson reveals the secret smile she reserves for people like me. Book people. "I'm so glad you asked," she says. "Come with me."

She leads me to familiar shelves, that special section I've wandered for years now. As I follow her down a row of books, my finger lightly brushes across the plastic covered spines, offering a silent hello.

"Try this," Mrs. Thompson says, pulling a book from the end of the shelf. "A debut. Quite the mystery."

I take the book from her hand and study the colorful cover. It's by an author I've never heard of before. By now I know that doesn't matter. She's taught me that a new author can be a wonderful surprise.

"Let me know what you think," Mrs. Thompson says, then nods toward the counter. "I've got customers."

As she hurries away, I carry the book to my secret nook at the back of the kid's section. A mystery. Like I need more of that! I plan to read until Dad and Zora come find me, but today I'm somehow distracted. Through the window, I see someone's umbrella blow inside out like something out of Mary Poppins. In the shopping center across the street, a man splashes to his car with a newspaper over his head.

I look down at my hand and see the ring on my finger. Girl Detective's ring. I put it on today hoping that somehow it might bring me closer to solving the mystery. At this point, I can use all the help I can get. *Keep following the clues!* she wrote.

And I just keep asking myself: *To where?*

9

"**HOW WOULD** we find out if somebody lived in the neighborhood in 1973?" I'm looking up at Mrs. Franklin, who's sitting on her lifeguard perch. Ally's beside me, holding on to the edge of the pool.

"There are some folks still here from back then," Mrs. Franklin answers. It's sunny again and the pool is full. Mrs. Franklin is an expert at answering your questions while keeping her eyes on the swimmers. "You could ask them."

"Like who?" Ally asks.

"Let me see." She thinks. "The Gateses. The Dentons. Oh, Mrs. Hale. She was definitely here."

The Gateses are an older couple who walk the big circle of the neighborhood every night. Mr. Gates waves at us with his walking stick whenever he passes. I don't know the Dentons. They must live up on Queen's Way. I know Mrs. Hale, of course, but it's unlikely she'll tell me anything about Ruthie Delgado.

"Or, I know," Mrs. Franklin says. "We could look at the clubhouse register." Next to the pool, there's a clubhouse for

Ping-Pong and stuff. "All the old registers are in there. We could look and see if there are any . . . what's the name?"

"Delgado," I say.

"We'll see if there are any Delgados listed in 1973. If it goes back that far."

I'm excited. This is the first real crack we've had in the case. "Can we look now?"

"When I have a break," she says. "I'll find you."

I say thanks, then turn to Ally. Ever since we got to the pool this morning, I've been telling her about the concert ticket and how my dad said it was never used. "Now we're getting somewhere."

"Maybe," Ally says, but not in her usual bright way.

"You worried about tomorrow?" I ask, a little guiltily. The play-offs start tomorrow and we still haven't solved her pitching mystery. Maybe I should be focusing on that instead of the unsolved case of Ruthie Delgado.

"Kind of. Coach still wants me to start but I don't know."

"Well, you've got to get back to normal sometime. And when you do, he wants you to be the one on the mound."

"I guess."

"What are you talking about?" We look up. Rose is standing above us at the side of the pool.

"You!" we say together.

"Ha," Rose says. She's wearing her new two-piece and I'm hoping a ton of sunscreen on that ghostly white belly. She jumps in, sinks to the bottom, then shoots up between us. "What's up, buttercups?"

I give her the ticket update but try to be brief. Ally's

probably had her fill of Ruthie Delgado and the unused ticket. Something behind me catches Rose's eye and I turn to see Romeo diving off the springboard. When he comes up, he waves at us.

Rose lifts herself out of the pool and says, "Come on." Before I can object, she's walking toward the deep end. I groan inside but follow because, well, I have to. Ally comes, too.

Romeo rests his elbows against the pool's edge and looks up at us. As Rose starts flirting with him, I want to run away. She'd hate me for letting her go on like this when I know he likes me, not her. But I say a cowardly nothing.

There's a loud creak from the springboard, followed by "CANNONBALL!" Joey Wachowski hits the water like an elephant, and the deep end explodes. Water flies everywhere.

"So juvenile." Rose wipes water from her eyes, casting daggers at Joey.

He ignores her. "Hey, Blondie. How are the butterflies?"

"What butterflies?" Ally asks.

"The ones in your stomach cuz you're going to lose tomorrow."

"You better shut that cakehole or—" Ally's about to jump in the pool after him when Romeo intervenes.

"Truce!" he says loudly, holding up a hand. "Just for today. Just for Sharks and Minnows."

Romeo looks at Ally, then eyeballs Joey. Nobody gives. "Come on," Romeo says. "You're ruining my summer!" That last remark was for Joey, not Ally, so Joey caves.

"All right," he says. "Just for today."

Ally nods. "Just for today."

Romeo gets Mrs. Franklin to shut down the deep end for diving so we can play Sharks and Minnows. Lots of kids join in, so there are probably twenty of us. I realize right away that I should have worked it out to be on Romeo's team, because every time he's a shark he comes after me, and Rose wants him to come after her.

After a couple of rounds of that, I claim a fake stomachache and lift out of the water. Romeo looks at me and I look back. Why doesn't he get it? Rose likes him, not me. Can't he tell?! I want to yell at him—*STOP!* Before *he* ruins *my* summer!

Grabbing my towel off a pool chair, I start drying my face and hair. Over the past five months, I've done a pretty good job of ignoring Romeo. We weren't in the same class at school, so we'd only see each other at recess or ball games and then always with friends. I've never said anything to him (or anyone) about the Valentine's note. I thought if I avoided him long enough, he'd get the message and start liking Rose. But he hasn't.

"Birdie." It's Mrs. Franklin. Looking back at the lifeguard stand, I see a teenage boy sitting there while she's on break. "Come on," she says, and I follow her to the clubhouse.

As I walk inside, everything goes dim. My eyes have to adjust to the inside light after the bright outside sun.

"Mrs. Franklin," I call out.

"In here!" The door to the storage closet behind the bar is open, so I head that way. Inside, Mrs. Franklin is standing on a ladder reaching for a box on a high shelf. "Help me with this."

I hurry over and grab the bottom of the box as it's coming down. It's heavy and we struggle to get it to the ground.

"Well," Mrs. Franklin says and claps her hands against each other. "If it's anywhere, it'll be here."

"You think?"

She shrugs, then bends down and removes the dusty lid. The box is filled with red leather-bound notebooks. Lots of them. On each spine is a date embossed in gold. Mrs. Franklin grabs one and holds the spine out to me. "Read."

"Huh?" I don't understand.

"Don't have my glasses," she says. "Read."

"Oh," I say and call out the date on the spine. "1984."

She digs deeper and pulls out another notebook. Holds it up. "1975."

"Close," she says and reaches in again. "What about this one?" She hands it to me.

"This is it: 1973."

"Okay," Mrs. Franklin says. "We're in business. Open it up. The club members should be listed in alphabetical order."

Sitting on the floor, I rest the book on my legs and open to page one. The title page reads: *Gainsborough Club Member Registry, 1973.* I flip through until I get to the *D*s and run my finger down the page. *Danner, Davis, Dearborn, Delgado.*

"Found it!" I exclaim, and look up at her.

"Great! Mystery solved. Read out the address. Then we'll see where it lands on the neighborhood map."

I run my finger horizontally across the page to the Delgados' address and stop. I don't need to look at the neighborhood map. I know this address. I know exactly where to find the house of Ruth Delgado.

10

LESS THAN an hour after finding the Delgados' address, we're standing on the front porch of 1917 Gainsborough Drive, ringing the bell.

How did I know where the house was without looking at the neighborhood map? Because there's a Japanese garden in the front of that house. Because I live at 1915 Gainsborough Drive, and if we lived here in 1973, Ruthie Delgado would have been my next-door neighbor.

The Delgados obviously don't live here anymore. The Gillans have lived here my whole life. They're retired and have three grown daughters who all live far away but visit sometimes.

I ring but no one answers the doorbell.

"They're not home," Rose says.

"Their car is here," I say and ring again.

Ally steps off the porch and looks at the fish in the koi pond. "Check out this one." She points at him. "Looks like someone gave him a black eye."

As we lean down to look, the front door opens.

"Hello, girls." Mrs. Gillan sounds surprised to see us but invites us in anyway.

As we sit down on the sofa, she turns down the soap opera that's playing on TV. Mrs. Gillan is older but not like Mrs. Hale. She wears exercise clothes a lot and I see her working in the Japanese garden almost every day. She brings us glasses of sweet tea and sits down in the chair across from us.

"To what do I owe the pleasure of this visit, girls?" she asks. "Do you want to feed the koi?"

"No, that's not it, Mrs. Gillan," I say. "But thanks. I'm sure Zora would love to feed them later."

"Well, send little Zora over," she says and smiles. She likes Zora.

"It's just . . ." I hesitate, not knowing exactly what to say.

Rose jumps in. "We were wondering: Do you remember the Delgados?"

Mrs. Gillan looks puzzled.

"You know," Rose continues, "the people you bought this house from?"

"The Delgados," Mrs. Gillan says, rolling the name around her brain. "We didn't buy the house from the Delgados. We bought the house from . . . I can never remember their name . . . Ray!"

"Yes?" Mr. Gillan's voice comes from his workshop. He's always making stuff.

"Come in here! Birdie and her little friends are here!"

While we wait for Mr. Gillan, I watch a man and woman start kissing on TV. By the time Mr. Gillan walks in, they're rolling onto a bed.

"Hi, girls," he says, wiping his hands with a rag. "Cut off that soap opera, Martha."

Mrs. Gillan turns to the TV and practically gasps. "Where's the clicker?" she asks like there's an emergency.

"I've got it," Mr. Gillan says, and the TV goes black.

"Oh, that *was* inappropriate," she says. "I'm sorry, girls."

"No biggie," Ally says and picks up an Oreo from a tray on the coffee table.

Everyone goes silent for an awkward moment.

"The house," Rose reminds her.

"Yes, the house. Who'd we buy the house from, Ray? It wasn't from the . . ." Mrs. Gillan looks to Rose.

"The Delgados."

"No, not the Delgados," Mr. Gillan says. "We bought this house from the Yukimotos. They only lived here for about six or seven years. I think he was transferred back to Japan."

Ally and I look at Rose. She pretends not to notice.

"Do you know anything about the Delgados?" I ask Mr. Gillan.

"That name sounds familiar. Did they live here before the Yukimotos?"

"Yes," I say.

"I'm sorry, I don't. Why do you ask?"

"Uh . . ."

"Kind of a neighborhood scavenger hunt thing," Rose says.

"That sounds like fun," says Mrs. Gillan.

"It is." Ally smiles, showing her Oreo-blackened teeth.

"The Yukimotos were really nice people," Mrs. Gillan

says. "They did such wonderful things to the house. Completely remodeled it. They're the ones who made the beautiful garden."

Well, that's at least one mystery solved. Now we know why there's a Japanese garden in the middle of our southern neighborhood.

"Okay, well, thanks." Rose starts to stand but I pull her back down again.

"Wait!" I say a little too loudly so everybody stares at me. *You know her address. Keep following the clues!* This is her address. *Was* her address. There's got to be something we're supposed to find here. Unless the Yukimotos destroyed any trace of Ruthie when they remodeled the house. "Did you ever hear anything about their daughter, Ruthie Delgado?" I ask. "She went missing back in 1973. We think she died." I can hear Rose quietly groan.

"That's terrible," Mrs. Gillan says. "No, I never heard that. What a sad thing to happen."

"Nothing left here of hers?" Their faces go blank. "You know, like a clue. Maybe a letter. Could be a cry for help. Or even a symbol of a cry for help. You know. Something like that."

They give me a look like I've just grown a horn out of my forehead. Mr. Gillan asks, "Do your parents know about this?"

"Oh, no. That's not the scavenger hunt part," Rose cuts in. "We just heard something at the pool about this Ruthie, and you know Birdie and her imagination." Rose flashes her smile that deflects adult questioning.

Mrs. Gillan smiles back. "Yes, we do. Don't we, Birdie?"

I feel myself blushing and take a sip of tea.

"What did you call him again?" Mrs. Gillan asks me.

"Oh, right. The imaginary monster who used to live in our backyard." Mr. Gillan laughs. "Oh, what was it, Birdie? You were so scared of him."

"Mr. Gotcha Man," I say quietly.

"That's right!" Mr. Gillan points at me like I just won a prize. "Mr. Gotcha Man. How could I forget that!"

"I don't remember Mr. Gotcha Man," Ally says.

"I was five."

"So imaginative. Even then," Mrs. Gillan says and beams at me.

"Daddy, don't let go!" Zora yells.

"I won't! Just keep pedaling!"

You would think a girl who wants to fly to Mars could ride a bike by now.

Ally, Rose, and I lie on the grass in my front yard looking up at the sky. It's after dinner—Ally ate with us because her mom was working late—and the sky is the color of a pale blue robin's egg. Lightning bugs disappear and reappear all around us. Dad is trying to teach Zora to ride a bike, again, on the driveway.

After we left the Gillans' house, we talked about the Ruthie Delgado case, and Rose and Ally think we've hit a dead end. So what if the Delgados lived next door a long time ago? How does that help us find out what happened?

A caterpillar walks across my hand and I let it.

"Maybe you're reading too much into this," Rose says.

"What are you talking about?" I turn over onto my elbows as the caterpillar slips into the grass.

"Remember that UFO you said you saw last summer?"

"Yes," I say. It was on a night much like this one and I remember it well.

"Do you really think it was a UFO?" Rose asks.

"Yes, I do!" I point above us where I definitely saw a UFO last summer. "It was right there. A triangle. It hovered there for almost a minute. Then, *bam*, it shot across the sky and disappeared. Just like that."

"Bird," Rose says, "have you ever thought that you see UFOs . . . and murder mysteries . . . where nobody else does?"

"Ruthie Delgado is not a figment of my imagination! We found the box together!"

"I know," she says. "Just saying."

Ally props up on her elbows. "Birdie's right. We found the box together. And if she said she saw a UFO, I believe her."

"Okay," Rose concedes. "If you say you saw a UFO last summer, I guess you saw a UFO last summer."

"Thank you," I say.

"You're welcome."

"Hey, guys." Ally sits up and holds her hand out, palm down. "Can we do the thing? You know, for my game tomorrow?"

"Yeah," I say and sit up, too. Rose joins us and we form a cross-legged circle. We haven't done the thing for a while now.

I put my hand over Ally's, and Rose puts hers over mine,

and we do it again so all of our hands fit together like a tower between us.

We look at one another. "I'll start," I say and take a breath. "With all the friendship power that runs between us." I look at Rose.

"And everything that makes our friendship bond," she says.

"This power of three that cannot be broken by distance or time," I say.

Rose continues. "That makes us more powerful than one."

"We give you, our best friend, all the power we have," I say.

"All our good fortune and aid," says Rose.

"So you can be . . ." I pause to find the right words. "So you can be Ally again. Queen of the pitcher's mound."

"Queen of the park."

"Queen of the world."

We gaze at one another and for this brief summer moment, everything is okay. Rose isn't moving. Ally isn't losing. And I'm not afraid of what's coming next.

"Us three forever," we say in unison, and throw our hands in the air, completing the ceremony.

Rose pulls out her phone and we lean in together. This selfie will surely end up on my corkboard. As we fall into one another happily, Zora screams with glee on the driveway. Dad yells triumphantly. We watch Zora pedal down the driveway all by herself, while the moon above us smiles.

The next day Ally pitches a practically perfect game. Rose

and I sit next to the General and cheer for her every step of the way. Ally, queen of the pitcher's mound, is back. And for the first time since the bet with the boys, I'm actually able to picture Joey Wachowski riding in the Fourth of July parade wearing a Hunters jersey.

11

EVERY NEIGHBORHOOD has a bad kid. The one everyone suspects when somebody's yard gets toilet papered or mail gets stolen. That kid in our neighborhood is Rufus Ledbetter.

Rufus Ledbetter is fourteen. When he rides his bike down the street, you better look out because if you're in his way, Rufus might run over you. We make it a practice to steer clear of him.

That's why, a few days later, I'm so surprised to see Rose talking to Rufus when I come back to the pool after lunch. He's sitting on one of the picnic tables outside the pool area and Rose is standing next to him. I watch him give her something, which she takes and stashes into her pocket.

"Hi," I say. They look startled to see me.

"Oh, hi," Rose says and pushes whatever it is deeper into her shorts pocket. Rufus hops off the table. "See ya, Rose. And good luck." He gives her a bad-boy grin, then turns and walks away.

Stunned, I stare after him, then turn to Rose. "What did

he give you?! What are you doing with Rufus Ledbetter, Rose?"

"Don't worry. It's not drugs or anything. Come on." She takes off behind the pool and I follow her. Within minutes, we're crossing the tree bridge to our island. We tag the willow tree like we're finishing a race before she finally looks at me.

"What's going on?" I demand while trying to catch my breath.

"Chill, Bird. Everything's good." I hate it when she says stuff like that. I wish Ally weren't at baseball practice, because I feel like I'm going to need her backup.

"Seriously? Rufus is bad news."

"He's not so bad. And he's useful for nefarious operations."

"Nefarious?" That's a big word for Rose. "What are you talking about?!"

"We're having another open house this Saturday and my mom didn't even tell me until this morning."

"Okay," I say tentatively, not knowing where this is leading.

"I've decided I'm not moving," she says defiantly. "And then I realized they can't make me."

Technically, they can make her, but I decide not to argue that point right now. Instead I ask, "So what are you going to do?"

"Good question. As I began to take matters into my own hands, I had a thought. If they can't sell the house, then we can't move."

I think about this for a moment. "Really?" I ask. "Do you really think it would stop you from moving?"

"Come on. At least it's worth a try." She reaches into her pocket and pulls out two small glass vials with some kind of liquid inside.

"What are those?"

Rose smiles. "Stink bombs."

"Stink bombs! For what?"

"So far we've been lucky. Three open houses and no buyers. I'm not willing to rely on luck anymore. So I was thinking. Nobody will want to even come inside our house once they get a whiff of this."

"That's got to be illegal or something."

"It's not. And it won't hurt anyone. It just makes wherever you are stink really bad. I saw it online. Some kid set one off in a school bus and videoed the whole thing. Everybody wanted off that bus, big-time! So then I had a thought. Who do I know who could get me one of these stink bombs?"

"Rufus," I say flatly.

"Rufus!" she says happily.

"Your parents will kill you."

"Only if they find out."

"Don't get caught," I whisper.

"I won't," Rose says and slips into the back door of her house.

I'm standing lookout for Rose, who is going inside of her own house to set off a stink bomb. How did I get here? As I feel my heart hammering, I wonder if the person driving the getaway car goes to jail for as long as the person who's actually robbing the bank.

I hadn't yet agreed to Rose's nefarious operation by the time of Ally's Saturday game. We had a whole conversation with Ally about it behind the concession stand before the game started.

"Come on, Al," Rose pleaded. "Reconsider."

"Are you crazy?" Ally exclaimed. "The General would kill me. And I don't mean kill me like your parents would 'kill' you. If only. No, this would be with a bullet and a shovel. There'd be no trace." She glared at us both. "So, no." And she stomped away.

A look of disbelief sprang up on Rose's face, so foreign that it made me laugh. It's rare that anyone says no to Rose so thoroughly.

We watched the game sitting next to the General and didn't say a word to each other. Mark wasn't there for the second week in a row because of summer soccer practice. And Ally played great. Maybe being mad at Rose made her throw even harder.

Between innings, when the General went to the concession stand, Rose leaned over and whispered to me. "Please."

I hit her leg. "No! I'm not doing it, either." I'd do almost anything for Rose, but this Nefarious Operation with Stink Bombs stuff was too much.

Ally won the game but we weren't celebrating. The General drove us to my house, Rose and I in the backseat and Ally in the front. I knew Ally was frowning, even though I couldn't see her face. "You girls are awfully quiet," the General said. "Are you okay, Ally?"

"Sure, Mom. I'm fine."

What a liar.

When we got to my driveway, Rose and I got out. "You coming, Al?" Rose asked.

Ally glared at her. "Can't. Got to clean up my room."

WHAT A LIAR. She would never do that voluntarily.

"That's a good idea," the General said. "You've had a big day anyway."

As they pulled out of the drive, Ally stared at Rose with such intensity I thought she might actually get through to her. Said the lookout man.

When we walked past Mrs. Hale's house, I asked, "Are you sure nobody's going to be there?"

"The open house starts at one, so only the real estate agent should be there. And she'll be upstairs or out front." Rose pulled out her phone and saw it was 12:45. "My parents will be gone by now. All you have to do is keep watch."

I stopped in the middle of the street. "Rose, this is so dumb."

She turned and said, "You want me to stay, don't you?"

We stood there staring at each other. Yes, I wanted her to stay! Of course, I wanted her to stay. The thought of going to middle school without her terrified me. And I knew that without a doubt, she'd help if I ever staged a Nefarious Operation of my own.

And I felt guilty about Romeo.

And she was standing there looking at me, needing her friend.

And that's how I became the lookout man.

I stand by the back door as Rose slips inside the house after using the key from under the hide-a-rock.

The plan is that Rose will tiptoe to the top of the basement stairs, break one vial (she's saving the other) with a small hammer that she left on the stairs, and open the basement door so that the stink can rise into the house. And ruin the open house.

In one sense, it's not a bad plan. It probably *will* ruin the open house. But when her parents find out, it will probably also ruin Rose's life. But Rose doesn't think ahead like that.

The door opens quietly. I look at Rose. She nods, but doesn't need to; the smell is already reaching my nose. "Oh, you stink," I say.

"I told you. Come on." We take off toward my house.

My mom and dad are cleaning out the garage, so it's easy to sneak upstairs. Rose takes a shower while I sit on the edge of my bed, waiting for the police to arrive.

It takes more than an hour for me to start breathing again. I don't ever want to be a lookout person again, but I'm beginning to think that maybe Rose got away with it. Maybe they'll think some random neighborhood kid set off a stink bomb in their house. Maybe Rufus Ledbetter. Why not? Everyone blames Rufus.

Then the doorbell rings. Three times. Urgently.

Rose's eyes and mine meet. We hear the murmuring of adult voices, then a loud, deep one booms up the stairs. "India Rose Ashcroft!" It's Rose's dad's voice. "India, you get down here right this minute!"

"Oh, crap," says Rose. He only calls her India when he's mad. She rolls off my bed and starts for the door, dead girl walking.

"India! Don't make me come up there!"

"Don't say a word, Bird," she pleads before opening the door. "Coming, Dad."

I follow her down the hall and watch as she walks down the stairs toward her red-faced father. Beside him stand my bewildered parents.

"You are in a world of trouble, young lady," Rose's dad says. "Your mother is out of her mind right now."

Even though Rose's dad is the one who gets loud and red-faced, he's not the scary one. That would be Rose's mother.

"I didn't do anything," Rose says, her voice so innocent even I almost believe her.

"Didn't do anything," he says. "Let's go." Then he sets his eyes on me. "Birdie, I hope you weren't part of this. And if you were, you have a lot of explaining to do to your parents."

Rose gives me one last look before being marched out the front door. As I hear the door close behind them, I see the look on my parents' faces. And I realize that Rose isn't the only one in a world of trouble.

12

"**IT WAS** dumb, I know, but you don't understand."

Mom sits at my desk with Peg Leg Fred in her lap. I'm across from her, sitting cross-legged on my bed.

"I understand more than you think, Birdie, but you're at the age when you have to make smarter decisions than this. You know better than to set off a stink bomb in someone's house. Even if Rose doesn't."

"But I didn't do it!"

"You didn't stop it. And that's almost as bad."

I stare at the floor. Her disappointed voice makes my stomach hurt. "I'm sorry," I say, and we sit there in silence.

"Okay," Mom says. "There are going to be people like Rose through your whole life, and you need to learn to stand up to them."

That's when I realize my mom doesn't get it at all. "I can stand up to Rose, Mom! That's not it. She didn't make me do it!"

"Then why *did* you do it?"

The truth is burning in my throat. Because Rose is going

to leave and I may never see her again. Because she was going to do it anyway and I didn't want her to have to do it alone. Because I am going to be a friendless freak without her and Ally at school next year. Because I'm sad and afraid. But all I say is, "I don't know."

"Is this about middle school?" she asks.

"Maybe," I mumble. "I'm going to be by myself. I'm not going to know anybody. I'm going to be . . ." The words drift off.

"What are you going to be?" she asks.

"I don't know." My eyes search hers. "Alone."

"Hmmm," she says. "You haven't been alone for a long time."

"And it's middle school and there'll be new kids and I just don't know how to do it without them."

Mom looks at me long and hard. "Is this because you look different than them?" She places her vanilla hand on my mocha knee and I know what she means.

"No!" I say. "I mean, I don't think so." It's true, where I go to school, most kids are white, but nobody cares much about things like that. Even in Atlanta. But I've been sandwiched in between my two white friends for a long time. Maybe without them, I will be different.

"I know we haven't made it simple for you and Zora. But we're always here to help you through any of it. You know that, right?"

"Yeah, I know. It's just . . . I don't know how to make friends anymore. Rose and Ally, they'll make new friends. Not because they're white. Because they're . . . Rose and Ally.

I'm not like them, Mom. I've already made my friends. It might be over for me."

"Oh, Birdie. You'll make friends. It came so easily for you with Ally and Rose. You're just out of practice. There're new friends waiting for you. New middle school friends."

"I don't want new middle school friends," I say quietly.

"You will." She hands me Peg Leg and stands up. "Now, listen. You're grounded. No pool, no friends. Our yard, our house. Until your birthday."

"Until my birthday! That's almost two weeks away!"

"Play with your sister and be a model citizen and you might get off early for good behavior. Okay?"

I can't believe it. We can't afford to lose two weeks! "But, Mom!" She doesn't say anything, just gives me that look that says *This is final.*

"Okay," I finally say.

Mom kisses me on the forehead. "It's going to be all right, little one. I promise."

"Mom?" I ask as she starts to leave. "I can still have my birthday sleepover, right?" It's been planned for months.

"Model citizens get sleepovers. Which might leave Rose out for quite some time."

Our yard. Our house. I am allowed to text Rose and Ally from my mom's phone to tell them not to come over or call until my birthday. I'm to have no contact other than this. Mom is going to talk to their mothers *if* there will be a sleepover. So I'm completely in the dark. I won't know how badly Rose gets punished. I won't know if Ally wins the game before the championships. And I won't know if I'm having a birthday.

During my first week of house arrest, I'm either reading in my room or playing with Zora in the front yard, trying to be a model citizen who deserves a birthday sleepover. I'm hoping to see Rose nonchalantly walking by our house, but that doesn't happen. So I have to assume that she's grounded, too.

I sit through every morning of Super Summer Mathematics Camp. I play every game we have in the house with Zora. I help Dad finish cleaning out the garage. And I daydream about Ruthie Delgado and Girl Detective.

It's the longest week of my life and it doesn't end the next Saturday. I plead with Mom, but she says my time isn't quite up yet. "What about my good behavior?" I ask.

"You'll remember this next time you think about setting off stink bombs," was her only reply.

So I miss Ally's game. I lie on my bed and picture her on the pitcher's mound, striking out boy after boy. Ally will catch a spider in a cup and take it outside, but when it comes to boys and baseball, she has no mercy.

On Monday, hallelujah! Dad takes Zora and me to the library. I practically kiss the sidewalk outside the library door I'm so happy to be there.

As we walk inside, I wave to Mrs. Thompson, who's checking out books at the counter. She sees me slip the book she recommended into the return bin and I give her a thumbs-up.

"Can we come see her, Dad?" I ask, pointing to the poster over Mrs. Thompson's head—the one about the author coming to sign books here in August.

Dad looks up at the face of Emily McAllister, who's smiling down at us. "I didn't know she was from Atlanta. That's pretty cool."

"You know who she is?"

"Sure. Emily McAllister is a big-time mystery writer. And coming to our local library." He grins at me. "Yes, we should definitely come."

I give him my first genuine smile in over a week.

As Dad takes Zora to the science section, I wander over to my section and start sifting through books, searching for something new. Finishing one row, I turn up the other and practically collide with Romeo.

"Hi," he says, equally surprised to see me.

"Oh, hi," I say, wishing I'd gone down the other row instead.

"How's it going?" he asks. He's got a Percy Jackson book in his hand, the one about the labyrinth.

"Okay, I guess." I look past him. Where are Dad and Zora when you need them?

"I was looking for you at Ally's game. She said you got grounded."

"Yeah," I say, then brighten. "How'd it go? What happened?"

"She won. Six to zip. She pitched a great game."

"I'm so glad," I say, relieved.

"Don't tell Joey, but me too. It's kind of fun to watch him freak out because a girl might be better than him."

I grin. "How'd you guys do?"

Mrs. Thompson walks by and puts her finger to her lips. "Shhh."

"Sorry," I say and we stay silent until she leaves the section.

"We won," he whispers. "But I think Joey's starting to get nervous. The middle school coach is coming to the championship game. He's going to scout them."

"That's awesome. Does Ally know?"

"I think so."

"She must be super excited."

"You'll be at the game, right?"

"Yes." I whisper. "I'll be there."

"Cool," he says and just stands there looking at me.

"Uh, listen," I finally say and look around. There's a girl from school at the end of the row. "Come with me." I lead him to the back of the kid's section. "I have to ask you something."

"Sure. Shoot."

I bite my bottom lip, then ask. "Do you like Rose?"

I can tell he wasn't expecting that question. "Uh, yeah, I guess. Rose is cool."

"No, I mean, do you *like her* like her?"

"I don't get it, Birdie. Didn't you get my Valentine's card?"

I start to blush. "Yeah, I got it but—"

"No, I don't like Rose. Not that way."

My mouth goes dry. "Yeah, but she—"

"I like you."

I don't know what to say. I feel all weird inside. So I play the eleven-year-old card. "I'm not old enough, Romeo. I'm not even into boys yet."

"I can wait," he whispers. "We're going to middle school together. It'll be fun."

"Okay," I say because that's all I can think of. I look pointedly at the clock on the wall. "I've got to go."

Dad's surprised when I find them and want to leave the library early. I never want to leave the library. On the way home, Zora leans forward in the backseat and loudly whispers, "Birdie's got a boyfriend."

I whip my head around. "Do not!"

"Do too! I saw you."

"Zora, quit sneaking around all the time!" I say and turn back toward the front.

"I won't tell your mom," Dad says, "but when you're grounded, I don't think you're supposed to talk to any friends."

"You mean *boy*friends, Dad," Zora adds.

"Zora!" I exclaim. "It was just some boy from school," I say to Dad. "And he was talking to me."

"So it begins," he says.

"What do you mean?"

"My little girls and boys talking to them." He shakes his head. "You know they're going to have to come through me first."

"Dad, I'm only eleven."

"You're almost twelve. Almost sixteen. I might start to cry."

"Daddy's going to cry?!" Zora shrieks from the backseat.

"Daddy's going to cry!" Dad yells, and even through I'm grounded and freaked-out by a boy, I can't help but laugh.

When we get home, Dad and Zora start making dinner. They usually cook dinner, and Mom and I usually clean up. I say I'm going to my room to read but that's not why I'm going there. I'm going there to look at the clue again.

Something about seeing that poster of the mystery writer reminds me that mysteries are supposed to be solved and the next clue is just waiting to be discovered. The trail feels cold but maybe it's not. Maybe I'm just missing something and it's my job to figure this out. Ruthie Delgado and Girl Detective are depending on it.

I pull the *Open If You Dare* box out from under my bed and unclasp the lid. There's the ring, the ticket, and the clue, right where I left them.

The ring. I don't think it's haunted like Ally does, but I'm still not sure why it's here. Did it belong to Ruthie or Girl Detective? And what does it mean? I place it on my book-shelf because if I see it every day, it might help me think of something.

The ticket. I reexamine the name scrawled across the back, Ruthie's name. But Ruthie didn't go to the Allman Brothers Band concert in 1973 because the ticket was never torn in half. So why is this significant?

The clue. I read it again:

R.D. is not alone anymore.
Because now I'm a dead girl, too.
I could have mailed this (I could have!) but

I'm not going to make it easy for you this time.
You know her address.
Where feathers are hard.
Keep following the clues!
Because he's still out there.

You're not making it easy for me is what I think. Especially if the next clue was destroyed when the Yukimotos remodeled the Gillans' house. And if it wasn't, it could be anywhere over there. As long as that's the right address. But it's the only address we have.

My room is at the front of our house and my side windows overlook the Gillans' front yard. My eyes scan the area: the front porch, the koi pond, the garage. Everything's new, or at least newish, over there. Nothing from 1973. As I lean back on my bed, I look at the haunted ring on my shelf and ask Girl Detective for help.

13

"I HATE that violin now," Rose says. "So much."

"You already hated it," I say.

"That wasn't hate. *This* is hate."

We're playing goofy golf. Ally, Rose, and I are on our own. Mom and Dad are playing a separate round with Zora. Because they do that kind of thing for me on my birthday! And my mom persuaded Mrs. Ashcroft to let Rose come to my sleepover!

Rose has been telling us her side of the fallout from the Nefarious Stink Bomb Operation: no phone, endless packing, infinite violin. Not to mention, she had to stay inside. She couldn't even leave the house without adult supervision.

"I'm sorry it was so bad," I say. Mine wasn't great but hers sounds worse.

Rose sighs. "We're moving. I can set off all the stink bombs in the world and it won't change that."

I rub my sneaker into the artificial turf. "I know."

"I knew all along," Ally says and taps her ball into the hole. "I hate that you both were so dumb that we missed out on almost two weeks of our summer. And you missed my game."

"You won, though," I say as cheerfully as I can.

"I know. But it's better when you're there."

We pick up and walk to the next hole. It's the miniature windmill that spins around so you have to time it right to get your ball through.

Rose goes first and a windmill blade blocks her ball. "Shoot," she says. "Can't I just move it?"

"Play fair," Ally says as her ball sails past the windmill to the far side of the hole.

Birthdays seem to make everything better. I'm twelve now and no longer grounded. When I looked into the mirror this morning, I couldn't help but wonder if I was somehow different. But then, when I saw Peg Leg Fred in the reflection propped up on my pillow, I realized I'm not that different yet.

Mom stayed home from work this morning and after we had Mickey pancakes with candles on top, she signaled to Zora, who ran off to the dining room.

"Now, you know you're not getting a phone yet," Mom said, eating her pancakes.

"I know, Mom. I know. I just wish I knew why."

"You know why," said Dad.

"Because phones are the devil?"

"I never said that," he said. "But I see it every day. All those kids on their phones. Constantly! If you get one too soon, your mind will melt before high school."

"Ta-da!" Zora ran back carrying a wrapped box and placed it on the table before me. I had no idea what it could be.

We ripped off the wrapping paper and I still had no idea what it was.

"It's a Polaroid camera," Mom said.

"Oh," I said, sort of curious. I'd heard about Polaroids.

"A relic from the Pre-iPhone Era," said Dad. "For pictures."

"And selfies," added Mom. "You watch the photo develop before your eyes. And no printing. You can post them on your corkboard right away."

I opened the box and took out the camera. Mom picked it up and snapped a photo of Zora and me. There was a weird cranking sound right before the camera spit out a picture-sized, plastic-looking rectangular thing. There was no photo, though, only a gray blank space within a little white plastic frame.

"I don't think it's working, Mom."

"Wait for it," Dad said. So Zora and I stared at the gray space as it slowly morphed into a full-fledged picture of us. "Cool!" I said. "Can I try?"

Later that night, after goofy golf, we take lots of Polaroid pictures. Zora tries to photobomb almost every one and it doesn't even bother me. I immediately pin three of them onto my corkboard.

There is birthday cake and the best picture of all is of Rose, Ally, and me behind a flaming mass of candles. As my family and best friends sing me the birthday song, I blow them out and make a wish that it can stay this way forever.

"I can't be as good as him; I have to be better than him. That's how it goes."

We're in our sleeping bags on my bedroom floor, stuffed so full with popcorn we can hardly breathe. The sleeping bags form a T at the foot of my bed, our faces in the center. It's dark except for the flashlight beam running between us.

"Cuz you're a girl?" I ask Ally.

"Cuz I'm a girl," she answers.

The championship game is this Saturday. "So be better than him," Rose says. "It can't be that hard. Joey's a moron."

"You better hope I'm better than him," Ally says. "Or it's your fault I'll be in the parade in a Broncos jersey."

"Yeah, please don't let that happen," Rose says.

"Yeah, please," I say and turn over in my sleeping bag. "Where do you think we'll be this time next year?" It's a morbid question but I can't help myself from asking.

"Ugh. London. It'll be summer and raining and cold," Rose says. "But you know what I'm going to do that's going to drive my mum crazy?"

"What?" Ally asks.

"Remain American."

"What do you mean?"

"You know how she hates that I have an American accent and mostly say American words and stuff like that?"

"Yeah," I say.

"She thinks when we move back to England, I'll get all

94

English again. I'll sound like I used to sound. Won't she be surprised when I don't?"

"You used to sound funny," Ally says.

"Well, I'm going to sound funny now in reverse, and this time I don't care what people think," Rose declares. She looks at us seriously. "Will you guys Skype me?"

"Yeah!" Ally says.

"Constantly," I add.

"Good," she says. "Where will you be a year from now?"

"I'll be right here," I say. I don't add the part about being friendless and afraid, scared that even Ally will drift away when we go to different middle schools.

"Me too," Ally says at exactly the right moment, making me feel better. "Maybe you can come visit us, Rose."

"Maybe," she says forcing a smile.

We get quiet and lie back on our pillows. I shine the flashlight on the ceiling and make a bunny rabbit shadow with my fingers, like my dad sometimes does with me and Zora.

After a while, Ally starts snoring lightly and Rose whispers, "Hey, Bird."

"What?" I whisper back.

"I'm sorry I got you in trouble. I really am."

She didn't have to say it but I'm glad she did. "I know."

It goes quiet again until she says, "You know what makes me sad?"

I could name a number of things but instead just ask, "What?"

"I wanted my first kiss to be with an American boy."

"Oh."

"Well, not just any American boy. With a certain American boy." She sits up. "I know you think that stuff is stupid. But my parents have put me on an accelerated kissing schedule. With the move and everything."

I slip out of my sleeping bag and walk to the front window.

"All that stuff is coming, Bird," she says gently. She knows I'm uncomfortable. But she only knows part of the reason why.

I look outside. The moon is shining down like a midnight sun. It strikes the maple tree my father planted when Zora was born and projects a creepy tree shadow across the yard. On the other side of the maple is our mailbox. Beyond that, I see the upper edge of the Gillans' front yard. Can't see the koi pond from here. Can only see their mailbox. Their mailbox with the bird on top.

The pieces start coming together before I can process them. I rush to my bed and pull out the clue box that's stashed underneath.

"What is it?" Rose asks as Ally stirs.

Opening the box, I pull out the clue. *I could have mailed this to you (I could have!).* I scan further down to: *You know her address. Where feathers are hard.* The words reverberate in my head. Then, flipping over the sheet, I point to the inky scratches under the words *I TOLD YOU SO.* To the little bird.

"That's it!" I exclaim, and hand Rose the clue as my eyes seek out my corkboard. Grabbing the flashlight, I aim it at my pictures and search for the selfie we took on the last day of school—the one in front of the Japanese garden, so close to the mailbox that the bird on top could practically peck us.

I shine the flashlight directly on the photograph. And there it is—the METAL BIRD, with feathers that are hard, right on top of the MAILBOX, in front of Ruthie's Delgado's house. Just like the clue says.

"What are you doing?" Rose whispers loudly.

Awakened, Ally stares at me, too. My fingers are tingling. My brain is on fire. It might be the only thing over there that escaped the Yukimotos' renovation. It's old, 1970s old. And somehow, it remains. That bird. I've seen it every single day of my life.

A bird in plain sight.

I take a private moment to let it sink in. Then I tell them. "I know where the next clue is."

14

WHEN WE sneak out of the house, the moon is so bright we don't need a flashlight, but we bring one anyway.

The Gillans' mailbox is made of brick, like a tall, narrow house, and the ancient metal bird is perched on top. The metal part of the box, where the mail actually goes in, looks like a small garage where the bird could park its car.

We stand side by side, staring at the bird with hard feathers. The street is empty and the Gillans' lights are out. "What do we do?" Ally whispers.

"I don't know," I say, crooking my head and looking more closely at the little bird. I try to move it but it doesn't budge.

"Maybe one of the bricks," Rose says and starts feeling around at the base of the mailbox. Ally and I join in. We touch every brick. All solid. Until I push the one right underneath the metal mailbox/bird garage. It moves.

"Look," I whisper. We bend down and I press at one side of the brick and watch as the other side slides forward. Carefully, I remove the brick.

"Flashlight," I say and Ally hands me the flashlight as I

give her the brick. I shine it into the space the brick left behind.

"What's in there?" Ally asks.

"Animal bones," Rose whispers.

"Cut it out, Rose." I bend down further and look inside the hole. There's a little compartment in there, a hollow space at the very center of the brick housing. The light from the flashlight is illuminating something. But I can't tell what it is.

I hand Rose the flashlight and start to reach inside.

"Stop!" she says.

I look up at her.

"Bones," she says. "Seriously."

"No bones." Even if there are bones, I don't care. I've come too far. I have to know. I reach in. The narrow hole swallows my hand and wrist before I touch anything. Thankfully, when I do make contact, it feels like a plastic bag. But there's something hard inside so I can't help but think there might be bones in there after all.

My fingers wrap around the plastic as the lights flip on in the Gillans' kitchen.

Rose kills the flashlight and we hurry through my yard and back inside the house. We're all breathing hard when we get back into my room and I close the door quietly behind us.

"That was close," Ally whispers as I place the plastic bag on my bed. It's folded over and stapled at the top. For a tense moment, we just stare at the bag, illuminated by the light of the moon coming through my window.

I click on the flashlight and examine it more closely. The plastic bag is white. We can't see through it. And none of us goes to touch it.

"This was your idea," Rose finally says.

She's right. If I hadn't figured it out, we never would have gone to the mailbox.

"Scissors," I say and Ally retrieves my scissors from the desk. Carefully, I grasp the top of the bag and snip off the top. I gaze up at my friends before pouring the contents out onto my bed.

Whatever it is is wrapped in an old dishcloth, held together with a rubber band.

"Okay . . . ," Rose says cautiously.

Slowly, I reach for the object. As I pick it up, the rubber band disintegrates in my hands. The dishcloth falls open. And it's worse than bones.

It's a knife.

"What?!" Ally gasps.

Not a long knife. Not a normal knife. A knife with a short blade that curves backward. Like when you Scotch-tape your nose up to look like a pig.

"This is so wrong," says Rose.

I hold up the knife and Rose hits it with the flashlight beam. "Have you guys ever seen anything like this before? What is it?"

"The police will know," Ally says.

"Is this the murder weapon?" Rose asks gravely. "Is this the knife that killed Ruthie Delgado?"

"It doesn't look like a murder weapon kind of knife," I say.

"How do you know what a murder weapon knife looks like?!" exclaims Ally.

"Shhhhh!" Rose shushes her.

Ally leans in and whispers, "How do you know?"

We all look at that strange curved-back blade again.

"I don't think it's the murder weapon, either," Rose says. "I mean, you could kill someone with any sort of blade as long as it's sharp, I guess. But it's not like regular murder-knives weren't available in 1973."

"Regular murder-knives?" Ally backs away from the bed. I notice she's still carrying the brick from the mailbox in her hand. "Al." I point at the brick.

She looks down, surprised it's there, then drops it on the bed. "Well, what was I supposed to do? We had to run."

"Something else is in there," Rose says, tilting her head to look into the bag.

I peek inside. "No way," I say and gently pull out a yellowed piece of folded notepaper. "The next clue." I unfold the paper and smooth it out on my bed. The writing is more faded than on the last clue. As Rose hits it with the flashlight, I clear my throat and begin reading:

> *Congratulations. You're smarter than you look.*
> *Now you know.*
> *Ruthie didn't go to see Gregg.*
> *Because of him.*
> *He knows how to use this.*
> *Of course he does!*
> *Find him and you can find her.*

Keep following the clues!
But here's the Wrinkle—
Meg is waiting.

Silently, we stare at the clue. Three pairs of eyes reaching back to 1973.

"Who's Meg?" I ask.

"Who's Gregg?" asks Rose.

"The Allman Brother," Ally says quietly. "You know, the one who lived." Somebody's been paying attention.

"None of that matters," says Rose. "Who is *he*? The one with the knife? The killer."

Ally squeals and springs away from my bookshelf like one of my books suddenly bit her.

"What's wrong?" I jump up and look behind her.

"That! Why do you have that thing out?" She points with a trembling finger at the black ring from the clue box that's been sitting on my shelf for the past two weeks. "Birdie, that ring is haunted!"

"No, it's not," I say before even thinking.

"No, it's not?!"

"Shhh," says Rose.

"First, we find a haunted ring," Ally hisses. "Now we find a killer's knife. You want this to be our last summer for real." She glares at me in a very un-Allylike way.

"It's not going to be our last summer together that way," Rose says. "Just in every other way."

PART 3

SOME OTHER
TWELVE-YEAR-OLD

15

IT'S THE day of the championship game. Rose and I are behind the concession stand when a man wearing a baseball cap and carrying a satchel passes us and walks up the stairs to the announcer's booth.

"That's Coach Rodriguez," Rose says quietly. "The old middle school coach. He was Simon's coach when he went there." That was before they built the new middle school and everyone in our neighborhood still went to the old one.

"Ally better be awesome today," I say. The knife almost ruined it. Ally was so freaked-out after we found it that she hardly slept at my slumber party. So yesterday, we didn't even mention the box or the knife or anything concerning the mystery. Instead, Rose and I spent the whole day focusing Ally on her number one priority: kicking Joey's butt and not wearing a Broncos jersey in the Fourth of July parade!

I did revisit the scene of the crime this morning, though. Mr. Gillan was replacing the missing brick from his mailbox. When I walked up, he said, "New brick doesn't match but I suppose it will have to do."

I felt bad because I knew the matching brick was upstairs in my bedroom, right beside the clue box under my bed. "It's not so bad," I said encouragingly.

He stood back, a cement-covered trowel in his hand. "Who would take a brick from a mailbox?" he asked and looked at me. "It's a strange world, Birdie."

If he only knew.

At the game, Rose and I sit in the bleachers next to the General, as usual. Mark's there, too, skipping soccer for the championships.

As Ally takes the pitcher's mound, everybody cheers loudly. There are high hopes and expectations in these stands.

Until Ally walks the first batter.

"Oh no," the General says.

"Come on, Ally!" Mark yells from beside their mom.

"What's going on, Simon?" Rose turns and looks at her brother, who's sitting behind us with his girlfriend, Ashley.

"Don't know. Could be nerves." Simon looks up at the announcer's booth, at Coach Rodriguez in his bird's-eye seat behind home plate. "Shake it off, Al!" he shouts.

As Romeo steps into the batter's box, Joey appears from the dugout, carrying three bats and a face full of intimidation. He steps into the on-deck circle taunting her. "Pitch-pitch-pitch-pitcher! Come on, Blondie, walk another one! Then I can bat 'em in!"

Ally throws the first pitch.

"Ball," the umpire calls.

"Way to throw, Blondie!" Joey yells. Ally must want to kill

him but she acts like he's not there. She throws again and almost hits Romeo, who ducks just in time.

"Ball two," the ump says.

The catcher stands and throws the ball back to her. "You can do it!" I yell as she steps back on the mound. "Strike him out!" Romeo pulls a face at me then turns back toward Ally, bat held high over his right shoulder.

She pitches. "Ball three."

"Come on, Ally!" the General calls out beside us.

Ally throws again and, "Ball four. Batter, take your base."

Romeo drops his bat and jogs toward first base while Rose starts quietly clapping. I grab her hand. "You can't do that," I whisper.

Joey drops two of the bats he's been swinging and carries the remaining one to home plate. He steps in the batter's box, digs in his cleats, and glares at Ally.

Ally's coach calls time-out and steps onto the field.

"I hope they don't take her out," the General says as we watch the coach and Ally confer on the mound.

"Maybe they should," Mark says from the other side of the General.

"Mark!" she exclaims.

"I just don't want that big guy to kill my sister."

After a minute, Ally nods and the coach goes back to the dugout. Everybody on our side starts to cheer. Mark yells, "You can do it, sis!"

Ally looks up at us then steps on the white rubber strip in the middle of the pitcher's mound. Her eyes sharply focus on home plate. On Joey.

She winds up and throws a hard one. Right down the middle. And *WHACK!* The ball comes off of Joey's bat fast and straight, like he's aiming for her. Ally can't get her glove up in time. The ball smacks her right in the face.

"Ally!" The General stands.

As the ball rolls down the pitcher's mound, Joey drops the bat and runs to first base. The catcher hurries to the ball and stops the third base runner from coming home. Ally's bent over, her hands to her cheek. If I were her, I'd be crying.

But I'm not Ally. And Ally's not me. As the General hurries down the bleachers, Ally straightens and holds her glove out to the catcher. He throws her the ball.

"She's going to have a real shiner," Simon says.

"He did that on purpose!" Rose exclaims. We start booing Joey from the stands and some of the other Hunters fans join in. "Jerk-bag!" she yells.

The coach walks out to the mound to check on Ally and the General isn't far behind. When Ally sees her mom coming, she waves her off, though. "I'm okay," she says.

"Are you sure?" the General asks.

"Mom, yes." Which translates to *Mom, get back to the bleachers, you're embarrassing me.*

"Does the little girl need her mommy?" Joey calls out from first base, and Ally's coach yells, "Come on, ump!"

The ump gives Joey a stern look while Ally nods to her coach, then prepares for the next batter.

She makes it through the inning. Nothing great. But nothing horrible. Two runs come in. At least Joey isn't allowed to score.

When the inning ends, we follow the General to the dugout and meet Ally outside.

"Put this on it." The General hands her a plastic bag filled with ice. "It'll take down the swelling."

Ally takes the ice and puts it against the side of her face. "Ouch!"

"Keep it on there," her mom says. "It's going to hurt."

Ally puts the ice back on and winces.

"You want to keep playing?" her mom asks.

"I do." Ally's eye looks awful but we all know Ally doesn't care about stuff like black eyes or bruises or even broken bones.

"All right," says the General. Maybe it's because Ally has four older brothers that her mom's that cool with it. My mom would be driving me to the hospital by now.

Over the next few innings, it's not bad but it's not good. Ally keeps pitching but only good enough to keep her from being pulled from the game. Joey, on the other hand, is pitching great. He even strikes out Ally when she's up to bat.

By the fourth inning, Ally's eye's grown deep purple and the Broncos lead 6–1.

"Ah, shoot!" We turn to Simon. He's looking up at the announcer's booth. Coach Rodriguez is walking down the back stairs.

"Maybe he's getting a drink," I say.

"Not with his stats satchel," Simon says. "He's out of here."

"Simon, get him to stay!" Rose pleads.

We watch as the coach heads to his car. "Don't think it would make a difference, Rose. Ally did not bring her A-game today."

As Ally walks back to the pitcher's mound, I see her watching the coach leave, too. I know she must feel terrible. This was her big chance and she blew it. But at least now she might pitch better. After Coach Rodriguez leaves, she doesn't pitch better, though. In fact, she might be even worse.

I drop my face into my hands. How can this be happening? Ally's never going to hear the end of this from Joey. She won't pitch in the big charity game. She might not get on the middle school team. And she's going to lose the Fourth of July parade bet!

I think back to that day in Rose's front yard when Simon and Ally were throwing. Simon had said that pitchers often have slumps because of something psychological. Something in their head. But if something in her head is causing the problem, what could it be?

Think, Birdie, think. It just doesn't make sense. Ally's been doing great again. The past three games have been solid. So what's so different about today? What made her go into the slump again?

I don't think it's the championship, because Ally usually shines under pressure. Joey is a pain but she's beaten him before, with pleasure. It could have been about being scouted by Coach Rodriguez, but then shouldn't she have improved after he left the ball field? And honestly, I don't think it's about the knife.

I squeeze my palms against my eyes willing my brain to find an answer. And suddenly, it appears.

"Mark!" My head pops up from my hands.

Ally's brother looks over at me. "What?"

"Come with me!" I bound down the bleachers and Rose comes after me. At the bottom, I look up and see Mark still sitting there.

"Come on!"

The General nudges him. "Go with them," she says.

Mark rolls his eyes and stands up. "Girls," he mutters but follows us anyway.

I lead them behind the concession stand, where Rose and I were talking before the game. When Mark rounds the corner, I confront him. "It's you, Mark. You're the reason Ally can't pitch today."

"What are you talking about, Birdie?" he asks.

"I know I'm right. Just listen. When was the last time you watched her play and she was good?"

Mark thinks for a second. "I don't know. She's been bad for a while now."

"No! She got good again! When you missed her games for soccer practice. Don't you get it? She's good when you're not here."

Rose glares at Mark. "What did you do to her?"

"I didn't do anything!" he says, but guiltily, like he's hiding something.

"Mark!" I say. "I can tell. You did something. You've got to tell us. For Ally!"

"Ah, crap," he says and kicks the ground.

"What?" Rose demands.

"Shhhh," Mark whispers. "Listen. I didn't think she heard me at the time but maybe she did."

"Heard what?" I ask.

"I don't know. It was weeks ago. Ethan was over and we were in my room." Ethan is Mark's best friend and they'd played on the same baseball team for years. "I was missing playing and Ethan was trying to get me to come back on the team. I told him I couldn't. But he kept bugging me about it, until I kind of exploded."

"Exploded, how?" I ask firmly.

"I said I couldn't play because my little sister was better than me. And it made me mad. And it wasn't fair. Stuff like that." He pauses. "But I yelled it. And I guess Ally was in her room."

"You mean in her room that is right next to your room," Rose says accusingly.

"Yeah. But it doesn't mean she heard me."

"Oh, she heard you," I say.

"I was just frustrated! I didn't think she'd fall apart or anything."

"Well, you were wrong," Rose tells him.

"She only falls apart when you're *there*," I say. "Because she's guilty. Ally'll let herself beat anybody at baseball, Mark. Except you."

He lowers his head for a moment and then looks up. "How do I fix it?"

Rose and I stand by the dugout waiting for Ally to finish up another mediocre inning. When she comes off the field, we grab her and send her to Mark, who's waiting outside the fence down the first baseline.

From the back of the dugout, Rose and I watch them.

While Mark talks, Ally studies the ground. When he finally stops, her head tilts up and they just stare at each other. Still as statues.

Rose and I watch them like they're a science experiment ready to blow.

Then Ally winds back like she's going to punch him hard. Her fist flies forward but slows as it lands on Mark's shoulder. Grabbing his arm, Mark pretends he's hurt like he used to do when they were younger. He pushes her. She pushes him back. In other words, the Lorenz family hug.

Over the last three innings, Ally goes back out there and plays like she's pitching for her life. She strikes out Joey twice and even though it's too late and the Hunters lose 8–6, Ally is back again. In those last innings, she does what she came to do. She pitches better than the boy.

16

"IT'S A skinning knife," I tell them.

"What?!" Ally says, hands covering her ears.

We're sitting on the island under the willow tree. Ally's eye is every shade of purple in the indigo rainbow. It looks like she was in a prize fight. And lost. After the game, we took a selfie together and Ally smiled big, in a way you wouldn't expect from a girl whose face looked like that. She didn't care. I printed the photo out last night and added it to my corkboard.

"How do you know?" Rose asks.

"Google."

"Sounds awful." Rose's face turns sour.

"It could be worse," I say. "It's for preparing meat, not killing anything."

"Still gross," says Rose. "So the question is, why was it there?"

"Why would our Girl Detective bury a knife that wasn't the murder weapon?" I ask.

"*Our* Girl Detective," Ally says. "I don't get it, Birdie. Why do you care so much? It's scary and weird."

That's probably a good question. Why do I care so much? Instead, I say, "I can't help thinking about the part of the clue where she says: *He knows how to use this. Of course he does!*"

"What about it?" Rose asks.

"I don't know. Why would she say that? *Of course he does!* has to mean something."

"Like he already uses the knife for something," Rose says.

"But what?" I ask. "Who prepares meat?"

"A butcher," Ally says flatly.

Yeah, she's right. I let this new intel sink in.

"So we should tell someone." Ally looks at Rose.

"What are you looking at me for? If we tell someone, it should probably be an adult, and adults suck right now. They make me play violin and move back to England."

"And I don't want to get grounded again," I say. "We're breaking the rules right now." I look around at our secret island, where we really shouldn't be.

"We don't have time for anybody to be grounded again," Rose states emphatically.

We look at Ally. She finally nods. "No, I guess we don't."

"I know I said I couldn't get away for the summer because of this work project, but your dad and I have been thinking."

I look up from my hamburger at my mom sitting across the table from me.

"Your grandma really wants to see you guys," Dad says from beside me.

"In Chicago?" I ask, an alarm going off inside.

"Yeah, my project is going faster than expected. We could drive up there at the end of the summer before school starts."

"No, Mom!" It comes out of my mouth too forcefully, too loud.

"Birdie!"

"But we can't!" I exclaim.

"Yes, we can," my mom says firmly.

"Everyone calm down," Dad says, holding up his hands between us.

"Yes, calm down," Zora mimics. I shoot her a look.

"We don't have time for that!" I say, searching their faces.

"Birdie, we always have time for your grandmother," Mom says. "Why would you say something like that?"

"Why can't she come here?"

"Because we said we would go there. We haven't been to Chicago in a long time."

"You already told her?"

"It's not until the end of the summer," Mom says.

"That's even worse!"

"I can't wait to go," pipes in Zora.

"You would," I say.

"Birdie!" Mom's eyebrow raises.

"Well, she would," I say and look down at my napkin.

"There are certain things we need to do in life," Dad says. "And hey, your grandma would be so sad to hear you talk this way."

"I want to see Grandma. It's not that. But it's the end of summer. Rose will be moving."

"You'll be able to say good-bye to her. Before you go," Mom says like it's not a big deal at all.

"You don't get it," I say quietly.

"I do," Mom says. "More than you think. But sometimes we have to look at the big picture. You have a family, too."

"Yeah, Birdie," Zora adds. "You have a family, too." I feel my face turn red. I want to scream at her.

Instead, I ask, "Can I be excused from the table, please?" As soon as my dad says yes, I'm out of my chair.

Outside on our front porch, I stare out at the neighborhood. Even after everything we said at the island about not telling our parents about Girl Detective and Ruthie Delgado, I had actually been considering it. Because I figured they might know what to do, might even be cool about the island thing, might want to help me. But what had I been thinking? They don't want to help me. They don't care what I'm feeling. They don't understand. They don't understand anything.

I see Mr. and Mrs. Gates crest the hill in front of me. They're walking down Chancery Lane, the street that dead ends in front of our house. Mr. Gates is carrying his walking stick, as always.

I watch them and don't watch them at the same time. Mrs. Franklin said they've lived in the neighborhood a long time. Maybe even as long as Mrs. Hale.

As the Gateses turn onto our street, Mr. Gates waves his stick at me. I half smile and half wave back. *The Gateses have lived here a long time. Maybe as long as Mrs. Hale . . .*

"Mr. and Mrs. Gates!" I yell, and leap off the porch and run across our front yard.

They stop and wait for me. "Hello, Birdie," Mrs. Gates says, smiling warmly.

"Hi," I say back.

"To what do we owe the pleasure, Miss Adams?" Mr. Gates says, tapping his stick on the asphalt.

"Um," I start, breathing harder than I'd like. "So, you've lived here a long time, right?"

"Moved here in the summer of 1961," Mr. Gates states as if for the record. "John F. Kennedy was president."

"Oh, okay," I say. "So did you know the Delgados? They lived here in 1973." And I point to the Gillans' house.

"Oh, yes," Mr. Gates says. "They were those Yankees."

"I remember," Mrs. Gates adds. "Moved here from Michigan. We hadn't had any Yankees in the neighborhood up until that time."

Yankees in the neighborhood? That was a big deal? I can't help but wonder what the Gateses thought when my parents moved in.

"I do remember something about their daughter," Mrs. Gates recalls.

"Ruthie?" I ask.

"I think so. What was it about her, Jim?"

"There was something," he says and looks up as if to pluck the memory from the sky. "I can't remember. Maybe some trouble. They didn't stay long."

They can't remember a girl's murder? Was that because

she was a Yankee and didn't matter or simply because they can't remember things anymore?

"Anything else?" Mrs. Gates asks, bringing me back from my thoughts.

"No," I say. "No, thanks."

Mr. Gates waves his stick and they start walking again. "Well, good night, young lady."

I turn to go back home then stop. "Wait!" I call out. They look back at me. "One more thing." I catch up and ask, "Was there a butcher shop around here in 1973?"

I see Mr. Gates thinking, but Mrs. Gates doesn't have to think at all. "Oh, yes! Smith and Sons in the shopping center. You know, across from the library. Where the fabric store is now. I used to go check out my book for the week and then pick up the best lamb chops. Delicious. Remember, Jim? Such a shame they closed. Nothing's like it used to be," she says. "That's a strange question, Birdie. Why do you ask?"

"Oh, just wondering. Kind of for a school project about the neighborhood." They ask me all about the fake school project, and I hate to lie to them but I do and smile until they are walking off again.

As I watch them go, I feel Girl Detective standing beside me, urging me forward. Sending me to Smith and Sons.

17

THE RAIN is pouring down. I can hardly see more than a few feet in front of me it's coming down so hard. I know it's not safe to hide under trees during thunderstorms but I squeeze against the trunk of the willow, trying to escape the monstrous drops ganging up in sheets, soaking me through.

Then I hear the scream. It's muffled beneath the rain, thunder, and lightning. But it's a scream. I know what a scream sounds like.

There's another one. More urgent this time. I push through the storm to the edge of the island to the rushing and roaring creek. And I see her. Coming my way.

A girl. Being carried downstream by the rushing current, struggling to keep her head above water, arms flailing. Her head dips under, then pops back up again. We lock eyes. I know she wants me to save her.

I search for a branch, a stick, anything to reach out with that she can grab on to. But there's nothing. I look back to the creek and witness her going under one more time. This time she doesn't come back up.

Panicking, I scan the raging water, knowing she's down there. Knowing she's passing me right now. I know it but I can't see her. The creek is a murky mud monster that has swallowed her whole. And it's not giving her up again.

I can let her drown. Or . . .

I can jump in.

The water's so cold as it sweeps me away. I'm blinded; it's impossible to see, but I swim down anyway.

I'm a good swimmer, I tell myself. I can hold my breath for a whole minute. Swimming deeper, I cast out my arms, trying to grab her. But the mud monster slips through my fingers like a liquidy ghost.

I swim deeper. And miraculously, begin to see. The water suddenly becomes clear and calm, while above, the mud monster rushes madly past. Below, where I am, all is still. Like I've entered into another world. And there she is.

The girl is floating at the bottom of the creek. Her eyes are closed, her long hair waving. I swim down. Hover before her. Recognize her.

As I do, her eyes spring open. Blue. So blue. Like Rose's eyes. Or my mom's.

I reach out my hand. I can pull her up. I can save her.

She reaches back. Gives me the faintest smile. As if she recognizes me, too.

Our fingers touch and—

"Birdie," she says. "Birdie."

Suddenly. Fiercely. Thunder cracks and the mud monster descends between us, pulling us savagely apart.

Her blue eyes are the last things I see.

"Birdie!"

My eyes fly open. I see Zora standing over me. In my bedroom. In my bed. It takes a moment before I can speak. "What?" I say hoarsely.

"Dad wants you."

Zora rarely gets screen time in the morning but this day is different. She's down in the family room watching *Adventure Time* while Dad sits at the kitchen table with me. Zora and Dad have already had breakfast, so he just watches me eat my cereal.

I try not to notice.

"They told me this was going to happen," he finally says. "But I didn't believe them."

"What are you talking about, Dad?"

"You know. How your wonderful kid who talks to you about everything suddenly stops talking and becomes a moody vampire for five to seven years. It happened to me but I was sure it could never happen to my Little Bird."

I sigh, somewhat teenagerlike. "I'm not a teenager yet."

He shrugs. "Okay. So something is really wrong or you've been bitten. And you know what we do to vampires."

"We give them extra cereal?" I ask with grin.

He doesn't grin back. "Or we stake 'em in the heart."

"Oh, yeah. I forgot that part." But we both know I didn't forget.

"So it's either that or you start talking."

"I'm not a vampire," I say, feeling my shoulders slump in that oh-so-teenage way.

"How can I be sure?"

There's a little mirror magnet that lives on our fridge. I grab it, then go and stand beside him. I'm taller than him since he's sitting down. "Look," I say, holding up the mirror in front of my face. "There I am. See."

He studies my reflection, then nods. "Well, that's a relief."

"Told you." If I had actually been a vampire, we couldn't have seen my reflection in the mirror.

He picks up an apple from the fruit bowl and takes a bite. "Well, then what is it?"

The dream I just woke from returns in a rush. The blue eyes. The muddy water. I know I'm sad about Rose leaving. I'm scared about going to middle school without Ally. But there's something else.

"I don't know, Dad."

He stops chewing and looks at me.

"Really," I say.

"You know I'm here when you figure it out. You can talk to me."

I nod.

"There are lots of vampires in high school," he says.

"Yeah, I know." He tells us a lot about the high school kids. How his job isn't only teaching mathematics. It's helping teenagers—the ones who've been bitten—come back to human again.

"I'll do whatever it takes," he says.

I know that, too. My dad would never give up on me. He'll always be there. I know I'm lucky because not everybody has a dad like that. Not everybody has a dad. But how can a dad, even a good one, know what it's like to be a twelve-year-old girl?

Half an hour later, as Zora talks and we pass by Mrs. Hale's house, I act like I'm listening but I'm not. I'm thinking about the girl at the bottom of the creek.

In my dream, I was so sure I recognized her. That she recognized me. But like wisps of wind that can't be caught, the dream slips away from me. I can barely see her face anymore. I hold tightly to the image of her blue, blue eyes.

I've got Zora pool duty this morning. After my behavior at the dinner table last night, it wasn't hard for Dad to press her onto me. Just Zora, no friends. So it's not so hard to ask him to drop off me and my friends at the library later in the afternoon. Only friends, no Zora. A fair trade.

This is the second time it's just me and Zora at the pool without a parent. When we did it the first time, earlier this summer, Dad had a little meeting with Mrs. Franklin first. They know I'm a good swimmer, but I don't think Dad would be comfortable unless someone like Mrs. Franklin was there looking out for us. When we enter the pool area, I spot Mrs. Franklin on the lifeguard stand and she gives us a wave.

Zora hates it when her feet can't touch the bottom of the pool. I try and tempt her out into deeper water, but she refuses. Stubbornly. So that keeps us working on strokes in the shallow end. Surrounded by little kids. Where the pee percentage is surely higher than the water percentage. Maybe

I should use this example when we work on percentages next time in Mathematics Camp.

While Zora swims freestyle (or tries), I pool-walk beside her. "Breathe, Zora," I say so she can hear me. She's actually not so bad at swimming, she's just really bad at breathing. So if she's not careful, the act of swimming itself could lead to drowning. "Turn your head!"

She doesn't until her head pops up with that familiar freaked-out look on her face. She's panting and struggling to tread water. "Help, Birdie."

"You can do it! Move your arms, pump your legs." But she doesn't and looks all helpless instead. "Come on," I say, trying to be encouraging. When I was her age, I was already on the swim team. I was swimming laps. I was thinking about jumping off the high dive.

"Birdie!"

I grab her and she wraps herself around me like she's a three-year-old. She's actually shaking. "It's okay."

"No, it's not. You were going to let me drown," she whimpers.

"I was not!"

"Were, too."

"Zora, I wouldn't. I would never let anything happen to you."

She releases her arms from around my shoulders (but not her legs from around my waist) and looks me right in the eyes. "You promise?"

Sometimes I wonder how this contradiction of a human

being ever became my sister. So confident in mathematics. So frightened of everything else. "I promise."

"Really?" she asks.

"Really."

Her face floods with happiness and she smiles at me. I can't help but give her some back.

Goofball.

18

THE OLD sign over the door reads FABRICS in big red letters. Rose pulls open the door and a *ding-dong* announces our arrival.

We step inside.

I've never been here before. My eyes flutter across the rows of rolled-up fabric of all colors and patterns before scanning the stained carpet beneath our feet. It looks like someone deliberately poured a trail of coffee from the front door to the checkout counter. The store is completely empty. Not a soul inside. Just a musty smell and weird instrumental music playing from a speaker somewhere in the ceiling.

"This was a butcher shop?" Rose asks. "Looks like it's been a fabric shop for at least a hundred years."

I'm agreeing with her in my mind when a shop clerk appears from the back. She carries a cup of coffee and takes her place behind the counter at the side of the store. "Can I help you girls?"

I sure hope so, because I thought we'd never get here.

After I swam with Zora, Dad drove us to the library. It

was only Rose and me because Ally has a sore throat. The General stayed home with her and everything. I think Ally wants to be sick because the Fourth of July is only five days away and she would probably rather die than wear Joey's Broncos jersey in the parade.

My dad waited and watched us go into the library. I waved from inside the door. As he drove away, I spotted the fabric store across the street in the shopping center. The fabric store that used to be Smith and Sons.

Rose and I were about to slip back out the library door when I heard Mrs. Thompson's voice. "Hi, girls. Coming in?" she asked from her perch behind the checkout counter.

"Hi, Mrs. Thompson," I said.

"Hi," said Rose.

"We just got in a couple of books I think you'll really like, Birdie." The librarian smiled brightly. "Give me just a minute."

As she went into the back room, I turned to Rose. "What do we do?"

"Play it cool," she said as Mrs. Thompson returned carrying a couple of books.

I love the books she's held aside for me. She knows exactly what I like and is always looking out for me. She is truly the perfect librarian. But I wanted to get to the fabric shop. We only had an hour before Dad would pick us up. And Rose had to get home for violin practice.

"Could you hold these for me?" I asked her. "We've got to do some work for a school project for a while."

"In the summer?"

"We want to get ahead," Rose answered. "They say middle school can be very challenging and we want to be prepared."

Rose is an expert at the Greater-Good lie. It gets the job done without hurting anyone. She's so convincing that I sometimes believe her. Mrs. Thompson swallowed it hook, line, and sinker, and smiled. "Of course. I'll keep these right up here. Just let me know when you're ready to check out."

I was ready to check out that very second and run over to the fabric store, but Rose pulled me toward the kid's section. "We've got to act normal," she whispered. "Librarians watch everything. And librarians tell parents. Come on."

We kept an eye on Mrs. Thompson, who didn't budge from her perch. "What about the back door?" Rose asked.

"Emergency exit. The alarm will go off."

"And we don't want that."

Minutes passed. We hovered in the spot where Romeo and I stood a couple of weeks before, and I half expected him to show up again. That would have been just perfect. Rose and Romeo. And me. As if she was reading my mind, she said, "Romeo gets back from Florida tomorrow."

"Oh." Me of the big words.

"I've really missed him," she whispered. "I think about him every night."

I didn't know what to say, so instead I started coughing. Not on purpose. It just happened.

"Bird, are you all right?" I nodded but couldn't answer. I wasn't dying or anything but I couldn't stop. Every eye in the library turned my way. "I'll get you some water," Rose said. I watched her scurry off, wishing deeply that she didn't like Romeo.

"Here." Returning, she handed me a Dixie cup of water, which I drank in one gulp. "You okay?"

"Yeah," I said, catching my breath.

"Then come on. The coast is clear."

Quietly, we hurried past the checkout counter and Mrs. Thompson's empty chair. She must have gone into the back room.

We crossed the busy street at the light and stepped onto the shopping center sidewalk. Past the Kroger, the Walgreens, the nail salon, the Chinese restaurant, and into the fabric store.

At the counter, the store clerk looks at us like she's bored and can't be bothered. On the wall behind her, hundreds of buttons stare back at us like the scary eyes in *Coraline*. Rose elbows my arm.

"Uh, yeah," I say to the store clerk. "This used to be a butcher's shop, right?"

"How would I know?" She looks like a grown-up but her tone suggests otherwise. "Lucy?" she yells, turning her head toward the back of the store.

We watch as Lucy, who is a grown-up, appears and walks slowly toward the counter. Lucy has gray hair and looks to be from the Mrs. Hale/Mrs. Gates generation.

"Did this used to be a butcher's shop?" the shop clerk asks.

"Yes, it did," Lucy says and turns her eyes on us. "Who's asking?"

"Hi," I say.

"Hello," says Lucy.

"I'm Rose. And this is Birdie. We're doing a school proj-ect about the way the neighborhood used to be."

"Isn't it summer?" Lucy asks.

"Yes, but we want to get ahead. It's for middle school, which we understand can be very challenging and we want to be prepared."

Good grief, Rose.

"Hello, Rose. And Birdie, is it?" Lucy says. "I used to know a Birdie in school. How about that?" She looks at us like that's important but I just smile. "Yes, this was a butcher shop. Back before all the newfangled stores came in."

I look around. Is she really calling this a newfangled store?

But then she tells us the story of Smith and Sons. About Henry Smith, who sold the best pork chops in northeast Atlanta. How he was the third generation of a family of butchers. And how everything was going right until it wasn't anymore.

"What do you mean?" I ask.

"Well, I don't know how much of this you can put in your report, but his son worked at the store. Think he started part-time during high school. Now, what was his name? Michael? No." She searches her memory. "Martin! That's it. Martin Smith. He was the son in Smith and Sons."

"What happened to him?" I ask.

"I don't rightly know but something. I think at one point he had to leave town." She gives me a grown-up stare. "I don't like to believe there are bad kids, Birdie, but that Martin, well . . . some say he was the devil himself."

"Really?" That seems rather extreme.

Lucy shrugs. "Well, maybe. Who can tell. And his father was such a nice man. Just don't know how those things happen. All I know is people were afraid of that boy."

"Do you remember when he had to leave town?" I ask and lean in. "Like what year?"

Lucy chuckles. "That was a long time back to remember an exact year. But let me think. It was soon after they closed the butcher shop. We moved in after that. About nineteen seventy . . ."

I watch her try to remember but I already know: 1973. So Martin Smith was bad. *But what would make a kid like that hurt Ruthie?* I think. There's got to be a reason. What if he liked Ruthie but she didn't like him? What if she made him angry? So angry he . . .

"Somebody told me poor Mr. Smith is in a nursing home in Decatur now," Lucy continues. "Poor soul. It's strange, though. One day there's a thriving butcher shop, and the next there's a For Rent sign out front."

I'm barely listening because my mind is going a million miles per minute. Of course, Smith and Sons closed suddenly. Because Henry Smith found out what his son did. He discovered that his son was a murderer. That's why Martin had to leave town suddenly. Maybe his father had to come up with some money fast to help him so he sold the butcher shop.

One thing they weren't expecting, though: Girl Detective. I look down at the floor and picture Girl Detective standing on this very spot, confronting Mr. Smith. Or maybe Martin himself.

"Wow." The word spills out of my mouth. Rose squeezes the skin at the end of my elbow. "What?" I ask.

She nods at the clock on the wall. "Gotta buzz." And she's right. My dad will be at the library any minute.

19

ALLY LOOKS miserable. I don't blame her. It's the Fourth of July—ninety degrees and humidity off the charts—and it's before ten in the morning.

But it's not the weather that's got her down, nor the sore throat. That got better two days ago. It's the convertible.

Joey Wachowski's dad owns a chain of dry cleaning stores, and he always rents an old-fashioned 1950s convertible to ride in the parade. It's decorated in red, white, and blue tassels and streamers with signs on each side that read: WACHOWSKI CLEANERS. Sometimes Mr. Wachowski rides in the convertible. Sometimes it's a local celebrity. Today, it's Ally.

The pool parking lot is a line of convertibles and parade floats. At the front, little kids on bikes are waiting to start. They always lead the parade around the circle of Queen's Way, to Chancery Lane, to Gainsborough Drive, and finally back to the pool.

It doesn't take long to spot Zora. She's to the side of the other bike riders, Dad close by. Last night, we decorated Zora's bike with red, white, and blue crepe paper, stickers, and flags. This is her first year to ride in the parade. I can't believe she's going to do it. But she and Dad have been practicing almost every night, so I'm hoping she won't run into anyone and bring the whole parade to a standstill.

Ally, Rose, and I are standing beside the Wachowski convertible when we see Joey coming our way. Flanked by Connor and Romeo, he's smiling so hard his mouth must hurt. They're all wearing their Broncos jerseys. "Blondie!" he yells.

"This sucks so hard," Ally mutters.

They walk up to us and stop. Three across from three. "Good to see you girls," Joey says, then aims his sights on Ally. "I thought you might not show up. But then I thought, Ally's cool. She'll be there."

"Is that supposed to be a compliment?" she asks.

Joey shrugs. "Yeah. Kind of." He points to the big jersey he's wearing with pride. "You're going to look awesome in this, Blondie!"

"I'm wearing that one?!"

"Of course. What else would you be wearing?"

"You've got to be kidding," Rose says. "She's not wearing your stinky, gross jersey."

Joey lifts his arm and sniffs his armpit. "Smells clean enough."

Rose, Ally, and I groan. "She's not doing this," Rose says.

"Yes, I am," Ally says. "Hand it over." Because that's how Ally does it. She knows in the world of baseball there is no crying and no welshing on bets. You do what you say you're going to do. Joey takes off his big Broncos jersey (thankfully, he's wearing a T-shirt underneath) and gives it to Ally. She pulls her enemy's blue shirt over her head and it completely swallows her. "Let's get this over with," she says miserably.

I pull her blond braids out from under the jersey, then we watch her climb into the backseat of the convertible.

"No, up there!" Joey points to the top edge of the back-seat, where the convertible top accordions onto the back of the car. "That's where you sit in a parade!"

Ally's jaw clenches as she slowly lifts herself onto the perch.

"And don't forget to wave," Joey adds happily.

"I feel so bad about this," Rose whispers in my ear.

"Me too," I say.

"Yeah, but it wasn't your big idea."

A whistle blows. Any moment, the parade will start moving.

I look up at Ally, her hands folded in her lap, her face so resolute. If it hadn't been for Ally, the three of us might not have even become friends.

Three weeks after Rose arrived from England, we weren't friends yet. Ally sat at the desk on my left and Rose had been assigned to the one on my right.

I didn't have any real friends in first grade. I knew some kids from kindergarten but I still felt like some dorky loner. Not a good feeling. Sometimes I wonder if Zora feels that way.

It was February and Bethany Hopkins passed a note back to Rose. Rose stared at that little note like it might be on fire and didn't move until Bethany whispered loudly, "Take it!"

As Rose grabbed the note, I recognized the handwriting

on the outside of it—the unmistakable scrawl of Billy Jones. Billy Jones was weird and sometimes mean. His notes had a reputation for bad words and getting the recipient in trouble.

While Ms. Hillbrook was writing on the blackboard, I found myself staring at Rose. She wasn't wearing her weird school uniform anymore. She looked pretty normal in a sweater and jeans, but the expression on her face told a different story. Like she was one kind of fish that got dumped into the tank of another kind of fish and she hadn't been able to breathe right ever since.

Whatever was in Billy Jones's note would have only made it worse.

I reached out my hand. "Give it to me," I whispered. She looked at me with her big blue eyes, confused, then relieved. She handed me the note.

"Passing notes is against the rules in this class!" Ms. Hillbrook had turned from the blackboard just in time to see us. "You know the rule."

I knew the rule. Whoever was associated with the note would have to miss recess and stay together in the classroom during that time. I had never been punished. Not ever in school or kindergarten. Frozen, I stared at Ms. Hillbrook as she approached.

Rose would get recess detention and so would I. And since Billy wrote the note, he would be there with us. Forty minutes in a room with Billy Jones! That was the worst punishment of all.

I heard a quiet whistle to my left and saw Ally's opened hand reach out. I didn't know what she was doing and I don't know why I gave her the note. But I did. And she ate it. Right in front of Ms. Hillbrook. It was the first of many times when Ally would save the day.

Instead of being stuck with Billy Jones in recess detention, I was stuck with Rose and Ally. As it would be from that day forward.

Now there's Ally, all alone on that convertible, and it just isn't right. The bikes start rolling out of the parking lot and the convertible begins to move. Ally would do anything for Rose or me. It was time for us to do something for her.

"Romeo! Give me your shirt!"

At first, he looks confused but then he grins and takes off his jersey. I turn to Connor and use my most compelling teacher/librarian voice. "You too, Gomez."

"What are you talking about? I'm not—"

"Give Birdie your shirt, Connor!" Romeo says.

"What? I don't get it. Why does she—"

"Just do it!"

"Okay, okay, Rome . . . but you can't tell me what to do." But apparently Romeo can, because Connor takes off his jersey and gives it to me.

"What's going on?" Joey asks, alarmed. "Better not be messing with our bet!"

"Nobody's messing with your bet," I say. Romeo hands me his jersey and in return gets a genuine smile from me. I pass it to Rose.

She looks at me like I'm crazy. "Just put it on, Rose!" It's Romeo's jersey so she does. I pull Connor's jersey over my head, then turn back to the boys. "See ya, fellas!" Then I grab Rose by the arm and say, "Come on!"

"Ally, stop the car!" I yell as we run after the moving vehicle. As she looks back and sees us, her face goes from night to day. The car stops just long enough for Rose and me to slither into the backseat and take our places on each side of our friend. The three of us, all in blue Broncos jerseys. In the parade together.

There's a crowd lined up along the street and in the pool courtyard the middle school band has begun playing "I'm a Yankee Doodle Dandy."

Ally beams. "What are you guys doing?!"

"Being patriotic!" I yell.

"Yeah," Rose shouts. "America rules!" She says this extra loud as we pass her house, her parents standing out front, the FOR SALE sign looming in the background.

We laugh and look back to see Joey Wachowski running behind us. His eyes say it all. Turns out, he's the loser today.

We ride through the neighborhood in the awesome convertible, dodging water guns and waving little American flags. The neighborhood is lined with hundreds of people. Not just from here, but from everywhere. Thomas Jefferson stands on the Declaration of Independence float behind us, shooting a water cannon into the crowd. It's so hot all the kids yell, "Hit me! Hit me!" As we crest the top of Queen's Way, I wave to Mr. and Mrs. Gates and look back to be sure trigger-happy Thomas J. doesn't hit them. And like a good founding father, he doesn't.

"Look!" Rose points toward Mrs. Franklin's yard. The boys—Joey, Romeo, and Connor—are running along, keeping up with us. "Romeo!" Rose yells. She starts waving madly, and Ally and I join in.

As Queen's Way curves into Chancery Lane, the steep street that dead-ends in front of our house, I see Zora's bike stall near the side of the road. Her anxious eyes look into the crowd. Even though the parade is moving at about three miles per hour, I know she's afraid of riding her bike down the hill. But she's holding up traffic, and some of the bigger kids start yelling. She's alone for what must be a heartbreaking moment for Zora, and I'm ready to jump out of the car to rescue her, when I see Dad. He appears out of the crowd like a superhero, grabs Zora and her bike, and pulls them to safety.

As we pass, I wave at them and smirk at their surprised faces. Ally leans into me and says, "Thanks, Birdie. This turned out great."

"Wait!" Rose shouts, and reaches into her pocket. We lean together and Rose takes our selfie. Us three, smiling, laughing, the queens of Queen's Way.

20

I KNOW it shouldn't be unusual to hear "The Star-Spangled Banner" on the Fourth of July but, trust me, it's an act of revolution when it comes of out Rose's violin at the Loser's Day party. From the first moment the bow hits the strings, I know she is doing it on purpose and I know she's causing trouble.

Rose's parents have hosted their Loser's Day party every Fourth of July since they moved here. At first I didn't understand why anyone would call a party on Independence Day (clearly a winner's day) a loser's party. But the Ashcrofts are not Americans. They're British—the ones we defeated to get that independence—so they are, in this case, the losers. And strangely, Rose's dad thinks this should be celebrated.

The backyard of Rose's house is decorated with twinkling lights and signs that read: LOSER'S DAY and WELCOME WINNERS. Lots of the neighborhood is there. None of us feel un-American by attending, even though the only flags flying are Union Jacks. That's the British flag. It's actually called the Union Flag, but Brits call it the Union Jack. *For Jack who?* I wonder.

The food is very strange, with names like Bubble and Squeak, Bangers and Mash, Toad in the Hole, Black Pudding (which is actually *blood* pudding, and isn't a pudding at all but a sausage), and Spotted Dick with custard (yep, that's its real name). Rose's parents don't make a big deal about it being counter-revolutionary. After all, they call it Loser's Day. They know who won. They know they're in America. They just want to give us a little flavor of their country. Oh, I'm sorry: *flavour*. And every year, we all think it's fun (except for the blood sausage part).

Rose no longer shares this opinion.

And this is her own little revolution. Each year Rose plays the British national anthem, "God Save the Queen," while we Americans boo (not too seriously) and Mr. and Mrs. Ashcroft sing proudly. But this year instead, full of the spirit of George Washington and Paul Revere, she's playing "The Star-Spangled Banner." I glance over at Rose's mother, her arms crossed by the barbecue. Fuming.

Yet Rose is playing beautifully, transforming our national anthem into a rebellious love song to her adopted home. Some of the American grown-ups place hands over their hearts. Ally leans into the General, her brothers Mark and James by her side. My mom puts her arm around me. Zora sits on Dad's shoulders. We all tend to forget (because she hates it so much) that Rose is a spectacular violinist.

When the last long note ends, everyone cheers. Rose smiles. Then looks at her mother defiantly.

As the sun goes down, the fireworks display from the pool begins. Everyone crowds into the Ashcroft's front yard and takes a place in a lawn chair or stretches out on a blanket in the soft grass. Little kids crawl into laps as the colorful show erupts in the night sky. Rose, Ally, and I sneak to the upstairs porch off Rose's parents' bedroom and watch by ourselves. We see Rose's brother, Simon, walk around the corner of the house with Ashley. I see Zora, sitting on Dad's lap, pointing to the sky.

"We're going to visit my grandma the week before school starts," I say. I've been meaning to tell them for a while now, but there hasn't seemed to be the right time.

"In Chicago?!" Ally exclaims.

"You mean before I leave?" Rose says.

"Yeah."

"But why? They know I'm moving, right? Don't they understand we need all of this summer?"

"I guess not," I say and feel a wave of sadness run between us.

"Can't you talk them out of it?" Rose asks.

I shake my head. "Tried. It's kind of a done deal."

"Oh," murmurs Rose.

"Gosh, Birdie," says Ally.

Quietly, we stare up at the sky. I'm relieved when Rose breaks the silence. "They don't do this where I'm going."

"What, no fireworks?" Ally asks.

"No. No Fourth of July."

"Oh." Ally sighs.

And I realize this will be our last Loser's Day party together. I may never enjoy the Fourth of July again.

"Will you have to wear a uniform at your new school?" Ally asks.

"Probably. Mum will be thrilled. She loves to watch me suffer."

I spot Mrs. Ashcroft among the crowd in the front yard. Rose's mom has always been nice to me, except after the stink bomb incident. But that seems to be behind us. I try and think when it started getting so tense between Rose and her mom. It can't have always been this way.

"My dad's moving . . ." A loud burst of fireworks drowns out Rose's voice.

"What?" Ally asks.

"Next weekend. My dad's moving." Rose says it loudly so we can hear, her eyes locked on the combusting sky.

It's only July and it's getting real now. In less than six weeks, Rose will be gone. In less time than that, I will be saying good-bye to her. Then someone else will be living in this house. And we'll be starting school, each of us, alone.

21

THE FIRST thing I learn is that Smith is a very common last name.

Ever since the fabric store, I can't get it out of my head that the father of murderous Martin Smith is living in a nursing home in Decatur. So I make a list of nursing homes I find on the Internet, sneak away to my room with the landline, and start calling.

The second thing I learn is that people who answer nursing home phones are, by and large, not so helpful.

But I keep calling. Each time I ask to be connected with Henry Smith. The first time I think I find him, I'm connected to a Harvey Smith, who sounds really mad that I made his phone ring. The second time, I end up talking to a man named Paul Smith, who is very pleasant. The third time, I get very excited because I reach an actual Henry Smith. But it turns out to be Henry Smith, retired lawyer, not retired butcher.

Finally, I hit the jackpot. When I ask for Henry Smith at the Shady Hills Retirement and Nursing Home, the receptionist says, "Yes, hold please," and I hold. Butterflies gather in my stomach as my call is transferred to Henry Smith's room. A lady answers the phone. "Hello."

"Is Henry Smith there?" I ask.

"Yes," she says. "But he's resting right now. May I help you with something?"

"Are you his wife?"

"No, I'm Clara," she says, a laugh in her voice. "I'm his nurse."

"Is this Henry Smith of Smith and Sons? I just want to be sure. I mean, is this the Henry Smith who used to be a butcher?"

She doesn't respond for a moment, then says, "Yes, I think so. I think Mr. Henry was a butcher. Can I take a message?"

I don't know what to say. I'm prepared to ask questions but not to answer them. "No," I say.

"Okay, but I'm sure he'd like to know who you are. He doesn't get many calls these—"

"Could we visit him?" I blurt out.

"Oh, well, it depends. I think I'd need your name for that."

"Sure," I say. "I'll call you back." And I hang up the phone. I just hang up the phone. In real life, I would make a terrible investigator.

The next day, I'm sitting at the kitchen table with Ally, Rose, and Zora at Mathematics Camp. But, today, it's not just mathematics. Today, we are cracking combinations.

I mean for lockers.

When you go to middle school, you get a locker for the

first time. Lots of kids have locker anxiety. It's practically an epidemic between elementary and middle school. As a teacher, my dad knows these things, so he's getting us ready.

Each of us (even Zora) has a combination lock in front of her on the kitchen table.

"I don't even know if they have lockers in England," Rose says.

"But if they do, you'll be prepared," Dad says. "And preparedness is one of the key elements to creating calm under pressure."

Rose shrugs her shoulders. I'm so glad she resists a "whatever."

"Here are your combinations." He hands each of us a small sheet of paper. I unfold mine and see three numbers inside: 15–22–4.

Dad explains how to turn the revolving lock: two revolutions to the right to the first number, one revolution to the left to the second number, and then straight to the last number.

"Done!" Zora's lock clicks open.

Even Rose, who's been giving us her best *I don't care* attitude, focuses harder. No one wants to get beat by a seven-year-old!

Click. I pull my lock open. So does Rose. We look at Ally, who's tugging on her lock trying to open it when clearly she's put in the combination wrong. My dad comes up behind her and starts helping.

My dad is very patient with Ally. He's the kind of teacher who makes you think you've figured it out all by yourself, when actually he's walked you through every step. After Ally turns the lock carefully to her third number, she gazes up at him. Dad smiles at her and nods. Ally pulls the lock. When it opens, her face floods with relief. "Thanks, Mr. Adams," she says.

"You're welcome, Ally. Now close your locks, and let's do it again."

Sometimes I think Ally purposely gets things wrong to get extra attention from my dad. It doesn't bother me. Really. I'm not even sure Ally knows she does it. But sometimes, when she just can't understand a mathematics problem (and it's really not that hard), it makes me wonder. Ally wants a dad and I've got a good one, so I get it. Even though sometimes I have to remind myself that it's important to be a good sharer.

"Birdie?" I look up. Everyone's finished opening their locks but me. "You want to join us?"

"Yeah. Sure, Dad."

While we're doing combinations, it starts to rain. Slow, easy drops at first, but soon it's pelting. I watch Rose's combination work slow as her eyes keep darting to the kitchen window.

"I read it rains all the time in England," I say.

"Great. Another reason I don't want to go."

"I don't know if anyplace rains like Georgia in July," Dad says. And as if on cue, a burst of thunder hits our roof like cannon fire. "Whoa! That was a big one." I tense up as Rose slips under the table. Dad looks down at her. "Rose, it's a scientific fact that thunder can't hurt you."

"But lightning can." We look at Zora like we can't believe she just said that. "Well, it can," she says.

"I guess no swimming today," Dad says.

"That's okay," I say. "We can hang out in my room."

"Me too?" Zora asks excitedly.

"No, Zora, let's stay downstairs," Rose says. "We could watch a movie or something."

"Yay!!" Zora careens down the stairs like she's won the lottery. "Which one?" she yells back to Rose.

"Whatever you want."

I eyeball Rose. "Are you kidding?"

"I want to watch a movie, all right?" she says defensively, when we all know she won't go upstairs because of the thunderstorm. I can't help but think, *Why today?* Because all I want is for us to go up to my room and start planning our secret mission to Decatur. Which I haven't told them about yet.

As *Frozen* starts on TV downstairs, I ask Ally to come upstairs with me. As we climb the stairs, she asks, "Do you have to wear that ring?"

I look down at Girl Detective's mood ring on my finger.

"It's not haunted." I hold it up, currently shining green.

"It's still weird."

"Think of it as an artifact," I say. "From another time."

"Great."

In my room, I pull the list of nursing homes out of my desk drawer and show it to Ally. Rose and I already told her about our excursion to the fabric store. She knows about Henry Smith. But neither one of them knows I've found him.

149

"Hmm," she says after I've given her a full update. "So you want to go all the way to Decatur and talk to some old guy in a nursing home who we've never met before?"

I nod. "Yes, I do."

Honestly, I'm expecting her to say that's ridiculous and there's no way we're following that trail. But that's not what happens. She just looks at me and says, "We can catch the bus by my house."

22

"I VOTED for president this morning. Did I tell you that?" he asks. "This is a very important election. Can't have a liberal commie in the White House. That's the way we ruin this country." He shakes his head. "Young people. Don't understand this voting at eighteen. Who says eighteen years old is old enough to vote?! You'll understand one day. Can't have a liberal commie in the White House. No, sir."

Henry Smith's eyes are aimed at me. Like I can vote or something. Like it's actually an election day.

I look over at Rose and Ally sitting on the small couch against the wall and mouth, *What's he talking about?*

Clara, the nurse, touches my shoulder as she pours Mr. Smith a glass of water. I'm sitting on the chair next to his bed. Because as Rose said, this was my big idea.

"Who'd you vote for this morning, Mr. Henry?" Clara says loudly. She hands him the glass of water and hovers like she's waiting for him to spill it.

"Nixon, of course!" he booms. "Who else would I vote for? Not that liberal commie, McGovern. I'll tell you that!"

"Nixon?" I ask, confused.

"Richard Milhous Nixon," he states emphatically. "Mark my words: By tonight, he'll be elected to his second term as president of these United States. Going to go down in history as one of the greatest presidents we've ever had."

We've studied lots of presidents at school and I don't remember Nixon being at the top of any great presidents lists.

I turn to Rose. "What year did Nixon beat McGovern?" I ask and she pulls out her phone.

"1972! What year do you think it is?" Mr. Smith says.

"Now, let's not get you agitated, Mr. Henry." Clara takes the glass from his hand. "These girls were kind enough to come visit. And I'm sure their parents have already cast their ballots for Mr. Nixon this morning." She winks at us. "Do you remember why they're here?"

Mr. Smith looks at her blankly. In the half hour since we've been here, this is the third time Clara has asked him this. And this is the third time he doesn't have an answer.

"These girls are here because you knew their grandmother when you used to have the butcher's shop. They're doing a report for school about how their neighborhood has changed over the years."

At least this was the story we came up with on the bus ride over. Ally figured out the whole bus schedule. We were supposed to be at her house for the day because it's Saturday and the General was supposed to be home but she's really working. And Mark doesn't care what we do. So we caught the bus on Ashford Dunwoody Road at 10:00 a.m., transferred twice, and reached Shady Hills Retirement and Nursing Home by 11:20 a.m.

At the reception desk, we acted like Mrs. Gates was Rose's grandmother and that she asked us to visit her old friend, Mr. Smith. It was pretty lame but I guess they're hard up for visitors at nursing homes. So after waiting several minutes, Clara appeared in the reception area and brought us to Mr. Smith's room.

The room is dreary but painted yellow, I guess to make an effort. Mr. Smith lies in a hospital bed, propped up so he can see us. A TV is bolted against the wall and the sole window looks out over a parking lot.

"Have you been to my butcher shop?" he asks, brightening.

"Yes," Rose says from the couch. "We went there the other day." She neglects to update him on the fabric shop development.

"Everything running like clockwork, I suppose," he says. "Can't wait to get out of here and back to work again."

"Rose's grandmother says you have the best pork chops in north Atlanta," I add.

"Just north Atlanta?" he says with a grin.

I shake my head, playing along. "No, I think you're right. She must have said all of Atlanta."

"Now that's more like it." His teeth are yellow but his smile is nice.

"Do you girls mind if I go check on Mrs. Landry next door for a few minutes?" Clara says quietly. "He won't be any trouble and it's sure nice for him to have the company."

"What'd you say?" Mr. Smith calls out.

"I'll be right back, Mr. Henry," Clara says. "Be nice to the girls."

We all watch Clara leave. I'm glad she's gone, because we have important questions to ask. But as the room falls silent, I'm not glad she's gone, too.

"Did you see Martin?" Mr. Smith finally asks.

"You mean your son?" I perk up in my chair.

"Yes. At the shop."

I turn to Ally and Rose, then back to Mr. Smith. "How is your son?"

"Martin is a good boy," he says, a twinge of sadness in his voice. "But I do worry. I worry about that boy."

He should be worried about him: He's a murderer! "Do you know who Ruthie Delgado was?" I ask him.

"Ruthie Delgado?"

"Yes. Did you know her?" I ask. "Did Martin know her?"

Mr. Smith leans up in bed. He doesn't say anything but just looks at me. Like maybe he's trying to remember something.

"Ruthie Delgado," I say louder. "Your son knew her. I think something happened to her. Do you remember what happened?"

"I remember you," he says, a fog lifting. "You. You asked me this before."

"I don't think so," I say, but he doesn't seem to hear me.

"About this Ruthie girl."

"No, I wasn't—"

"You. I remember you." He's staring at me like he's in a trance. "Red hair. You had red hair. Is that a wig you're wearing?"

I touch my dark hair. This is getting weird.

"I remember you," he says again. "Why are you hiding your hair? Why are you trying to trick me?"

I don't know what he's talking about. "I just wanted to know about Martin," I say nervously. "And Ruthie Delgado? What did he do to her? And then what did he do to the girl who came asking?"

"Martin!" he calls out. "Martin, she's here again! I won't let them hurt you, Martin."

I look back at Ally and Rose, who are already standing, their shocked faces matching mine. My hair isn't red. I'm not trying to trick him. And then it hits me. He's not remembering me. He's remembering her.

He's remembering some other twelve-year-old.

"Mr. Henry, calm down, now." I jump to my feet as Clara sails back into the room. "It's okay. You just got confused." She helps him settle back in bed. "Maybe it's time for a little rest."

"I don't know. I just don't know," he says.

I hover at the doorway and watch the fog reclaim him. Ally and Rose are already fleeing down the hall.

"There, there," Clara says, pulling up his blanket. "It's Clara, Mr. Henry. Remember me? Clara."

He's very still for a long moment, then asks, "Have I voted yet today, Clara?"

"Yes, you have. Voted first thing this morning."

"Good." He lifts his head and looks at me. "And thank you, Clara, for having your daughter come visit with me today. She's nice like you."

"She sure enjoyed visiting with you, too." She pats his shoulder and says, "Just rest now. Just rest."

It's strange that he thinks Clara is my mother. Our skin is almost the same color but we look nothing alike. And she's way too old to be my mom. After Mr. Smith closes his eyes, Clara walks toward me.

"He's a nice old white man," she says quietly. "But he doesn't much remember progress, if you get what I mean." She gives me a questioning look. "He didn't say anything he shouldn't have, did he?"

I shake my head. I see my white friends waiting down the hall and know Clara would never ask them that. "No, he didn't," I say.

"Good." Clara gives me a smile. I look at my friends again and then turn back to her. Clara must know things.

"Can I ask you a question?"

"Yes, of course," she says.

"Do you know what happened to his son, Martin?"

"Oh, Martin. Mr. Henry gets upset when people bring up Martin."

"Why?"

"Well, because Martin died," she said. "When he was young, too."

"How did it happen?"

"I don't know. Some kind of accident," Clara says, then stops. I think she's finished talking but she's not. "I hear things, you know. Over the years you can't help but hear what people say. I get the idea that Martin was a bad egg." She pauses again and her eyes meet mine. "I'd bet dollars to doughnuts that boy met with trouble."

Martin is dead. I stand there staring at Clara, not knowing what else to say. I wasn't expecting this. How can you solve a murder mystery when the murderer is dead?

I tell Rose and Ally what Clara told me on the bus ride home and they look, well, relieved.

"I'm glad it's over," Ally says.

"Yeah, but it's actually not. We don't know exactly what happened," I say.

"We know something bad happened to Ruthie Delgado and to some weird girl who buried clues for a living," Rose says. "He's dead. They're dead. Do we have to know the details?"

"I really don't want to know the details," Ally says. "And meeting that old guy was . . ."

"Disturbing." Rose fills in the blank.

I agree. Meeting Henry Smith *was* disturbing. But I don't say it.

Ally and I are sitting together and Rose is leaning over the seat in front of us.

"We came all this way, Bird," Rose says. "I know you wanted to figure this out but we may never figure it out. It's kind of a dead end and, well . . ."

"But didn't you see," I say, "he thought I was her."

"Who?" Ally asks.

"Mr. Smith. He thought I was Girl Detective."

They glance at each other.

"She must have had red hair," I say. "She must have come

to see him about Martin. Maybe confronted him. Don't you get it? She was our age. Just a girl. And then someone killed her."

They stare at me until Ally's eyes drop. "I wish we never found that dumb box," she says.

My eyes dart to Rose. "It was a long time ago," she says with a shrug.

"But what does that matter?!"

Rose sneaks a look at Ally. "I guess what we're saying is . . ."

"Can we be done now?" Ally's words prick like needles on my skin. *Can we be done now? Seriously?*

"Sure," I manage. Because what else can I say? As weird as the trip to Decatur was, it solved part of the mystery. Could that be enough?

As we fall into an awkward silence, I stare out the bus window. The telephone poles, passing one after the other, blend together, and I can't stop thinking about the girl who came before me, the girl who must have had red hair and who must have questioned Mr. Smith about Ruthie Delgado's murder, too. Mr. Smith thought I was some other twelve-year-old. He thought I was Girl Detective.

And even though I may never know what happened to Ruthie Delgado, I feel a deep desire to solve the mystery of her. Was Girl Detective the drowning girl with the waving hair in my dream? The girl with blue eyes who I couldn't save? I look down at the mood ring on my finger, now also blue, and wonder if she wore this ring when she faced Henry Smith all those years ago. Whether my friends want to help or not, I need to solve the mystery of this girl. The girl from the past who is somehow like me.

PART 4

MEG IS WAITING

23

THE FUNERAL procession is quite orderly, considering.

"You really think this is an appropriate response?" Ally asks.

Rose spins around, eyes blazing. "Yes, I think it's an appropriate response! It's the only response as far as I'm concerned!"

I decide to say nothing and just watch the rising flames float downstream. A Viking funeral in the middle of July.

This was a bad idea.

It started on the afternoon after the nursing home. After we got back from our journey, Rose called her mom from Ally's house to ask if she could spend the night. My parents were fine with it, but Rose's mom said Rose had to come home to practice first. As Ally and I listened, what began as a regular conversation escalated into a full-on battle. I could never imagine speaking to my mom like that. Or vice versa.

Twenty minutes later, Rose's mom showed up. She

marched Rose out of Ally's house and we didn't hear from her for three whole days.

Rose showed up at Mathematics Camp on Tuesday like nothing had happened. She was carrying a backpack, though, and that was unusual. Especially because she didn't open it or refer to it in any way.

Later, on the way to the pool, Rose still hadn't said anything about the backpack over her shoulders. As we passed Mrs. Hale's house, I reached my breaking point. "What's with the backpack, Rose?"

"You'll see," she said, her blue eyes twinkling in the bright sun.

As we approached the pool, her pace quickened. We passed by the pool courtyard and descended onto the path that led to the woods. This was the first time in our lives that Ally and I struggled to keep up with her.

Once in the woods, we followed Rose downstream. I assumed we were heading for our island but when we passed the tree bridge and left our island behind, I glanced back at Ally. "Where are we going?"

"Almost there." Rose marched on, our personal pied piper. Weaving through trees and brush, she hiked on, her backpack bouncing every step of the way.

Downstream, the creek became flat and calm. The water flowed evenly under lush green tree limbs that draped overhead.

Rose finally stopped when we hit the little beach at the shallows. It's not a real beach with waves or sharks or anything. But it's sandy and the closest thing this muddy creek will ever have to one. We've been here before but not in a long time. She dropped her backpack on the sand. "We're here."

"What's with all the mystery?" I asked.

Rose kneeled down beside the backpack. "My parents sold the house, I hate my mum, and I'm never playing the violin again."

"Oh, crap," Ally said.

"Al, you're a poet," said Rose. "Couldn't have said it better myself."

Ally and I catch each other's eyes. We fall on our knees in the sand beside her.

"There's no getting out of this. I'm definitely going back to England."

We sat there silently, leaves rustling above. "We're really going to miss you," I said.

"Yeah," added Ally. "A lot."

Rose tried to smile. "I'm going to miss you squares, too. But I was thinking, I'm kind of an American now. And when Americans are fed up, we do things like the Boston Tea Party. Acts of rebellion are in our blood. We throw things off boats. We burn things." She eyed us both, then said, "And on that note . . ."

She unzipped the backpack and pulled out her violin. Solemnly, she said, "I'm not taking everything with me."

"What are you doing, Rose?" I asked warily.

Rose looked us as calmly. Too calmly. "Don't worry. Not all things were meant to last."

She laid her violin reverently on the sand. She reached in

the backpack again, pulled out a hammer, and smashed a hole right in the middle of it. The strings whined and groaned. One popped off completely.

"Dude!" Ally shouted.

"It's okay," Rose said. "It's like a Band-Aid. Had to be ripped off."

Stunned, Ally and I just watched as she pulled more supplies from her backpack. Some newspaper. A box of matches. A bottle of lighter fluid.

"What the—" I almost said a bad word. I stopped myself, but seriously, Rose. Lighter fluid?

"It's just from the grill. There's hardly any left." She handed me the metal container. "Here, shake it."

"That's not the point." But I shook it anyway. She was telling the truth. "But it's lighter fluid! That is against the rules!"

"It is," Ally echoed.

"I know," Rose said. "And I promise, I'll never do it again. Just this once."

We watched Rose fill the hollow violin with crumpled newspaper. Then we watched her shower the newspaper with lighter fluid. And I thought this: *As much as I will miss Rose, and I will miss her so much, in some ways it might be better if she goes. Because it's hard for me to say no to her even when she does questionable things. We aren't even in middle school yet and she is about to set a fire using lighter fluid. What will she be like in high school?*

Rose grabbed a match and held it up defiantly. "The tyranny I have lived under and by extension, you, my dearest friends, have had to endure is coming to an end."

I felt Ally sneaking a peek at me. I dared not look back.

"Today marks the end of Mum's rule," she said, and went to strike the match.

"Wait!" I exclaimed. Rose stopped and stared at me. "If you kill yourself, I'm going to be really mad at you."

Rose nodded. "That's fair, Bird." Her lips turned up slightly. "Totally fair." Then she slid the match against the matchbox. It ignited, combusting in blue, red, then orange. She grabbed the long neck of her violin and lowered the body of the broken, lighter-fluid soaked instrument into the creek. As she pushed the violin from shore, she tossed out the burning match and, like something out of a Norse legend, the flame hit the target.

Whoosh. The violin practically exploded in flames. We leaned back, surprised by its fast fury.

"Lighter fluid really works," Ally said.

"Yeah," was all I could manage.

The current claimed the burning violin like a wooden ship pushing out to sea. This is how the Vikings did it. In old Norse times, they would place a dead warrior or nobleman on a ship laden with wood (no lighter fluid in those days), send it out to sea, and set it ablaze, sometimes by shooting it with a flaming arrow. The dead guy wasn't alone on that floating funeral pyre, though. His treasures from life went with him to keep him company on his way to Valhalla (the home of the gods).

As black smoke unfurls from the burning pyre that used to be Rose's violin, I wonder what treasure is being sacrificed with it. I fear we are witnessing Rose's love of music, her innate talent, floating away, too. Floating to Valhalla. And I wonder if, someday, Rose will regret this.

We watch the burning violin grow smaller and smaller. As it disappears around the curve in the creek, I can speak again. "What will you tell her?"

"Not sure." Rose says, her eyes fixed downstream. "Maybe I'll say I lost it."

"She won't believe you," says Ally.

"I know."

24

IT'S BEEN three days since the Viking funeral, and this is how Rose decided to play it. The first day after the violin was gone, Rose acted like she couldn't find it and pretended to be very distressed. The next day (yesterday) she doubled down on her lie. Since her mom doesn't always lock the front door and Rose practices in the front living room, Rose announced that her violin must have been stolen. And that it was her mom's fault for leaving the door unlocked!

Breathtaking.

Today, the three of us have been at the pool all morning, mostly talking about the violin incident while standing shoulder-deep in pool water. When Ally points behind me, I turn and see Dad walking toward us. He's got Zora by the hand. She's wearing a bathing suit, and he's not. I know what this means.

"Just an hour," he says, looking down at me, Ally, and Rose. "It's good babysitting experience—for all of you."

"Birdie!" Zora screams, and jumps in wildly.

As she sinks to the bottom, Ally pulls her up with one

hand. "It's too deep here. Let's go where you can touch the bottom."

I squint up at Dad. "Okay. I've got it."

Dad looks at Ally, then back at me. "Well somebody's got it."

Playfully, I splash him. "We'll see you at lunch." He waves at Mrs. Franklin sitting on the lifeguard stand and points toward us. She waves back and gives him a thumbs-up. Before he leaves, though, he turns to me seriously and says, "Remember, you're in charge."

I'm a model big sister for at least an hour. We play Marco Polo and Underwater Tea Party. I help Zora practice swim strokes and everything.

Then Joey starts up. "You coming to the big game, Blondie?" He drops this little bomb while he, Romeo, and Connor walk past toward the deep end.

Ally seethes.

Joey is psyched about the charity game. Partly because everyone at the ballpark attends and winning the big charity game somewhat assures his position as the sixth-grade middle school pitcher. And partly because he gets to torture Ally with it.

"Come on," Rose says, and Ally follows her out of the water. "Who died and left you king of the jerks," I hear Rose yell at Joey from across the pool.

For just a minute, I get out of the pool to join them, leaving Zora playing happily on the shallow steps.

"King of the jerks?!" Joey exclaims. "I'm king of the

mound." He looks at Ally pointedly. "Cuz only kings, not queens, belong there."

Okay, that's enough! I glare at Romeo, who reaches his arm out casually and pushes Joey into the pool.

We all laugh—me, Rose, Ally, Romeo, even Connor. Not Joey. He pops up from the water like a hissing snake and is out of the pool in seconds. "You're dead, Romeo!"

Romeo smirks, but as Joey's feet hit the concrete, Romeo starts to run. He circles the deep end, sailing past the diving boards, Joey on his tail.

A loud whistle blasts and instantly, they downshift to fast-walking. "No running," Mrs. Franklin shouts from the high lifeguard's chair.

"We're not running," Joey cries defensively, and walks faster.

She blows the whistle again. "Mr. Wachowski! Stop moving now!"

Joey obeys but I can see it's killing him. Romeo walks on, turns the corner of the pool, and glances back at Joey nonchalantly.

"It's not fair," I hear Joey whine while I watch Romeo, not a care in the world, stroll along the other side of the pool, on his way back to us.

As Joey sits in "tween time-out" by the side of Mrs. Franklin's lifeguard chair, his feet dangling in the water, Romeo rejoins us. He waves at Joey, tauntingly, and Joey groans. Ally waves, too, a big smirk on her face, then we all join in, laughing and smiling. Poor Joey.

"You never get in trouble," I say to Romeo. It's true. He hangs out with the most troublemaking boy in school but trouble never sticks to him.

He smiles broadly and shrugs. "Don't know. Maybe Joey's just a bigger target."

"Much bigger," Rose quips.

Ally cocks her head and looks thoughtfully at Joey. "But look at him, all sad and in time-out. He's kind of cute."

"For a big-boned boy."

"Come on, Rose," I say.

"Yes, Miss Adams," she teases, and I feel my face turning red.

Rose whispers, "Blush much?"

I whip around. "I am not blushing!"

"Are, too!"

My eyes are steaming. I want to be mad at Rose, but she's right. I am blushing. Because Rose called out my teacher voice in front of Romeo.

Suddenly, I'm done with swimming. Done with all of it. It's got to be lunchtime by now. I walk toward the shallows to pick up Zora.

"Where are you going?" Rose calls out. "Come on. Don't be mad."

"I'm not mad. I'm hungry."

Rose catches up with me. "Don't be a liar."

I stop and turn to her. "You're calling me the liar? That's hilarious, Rose."

"I don't lie to you." Even though I've seen her lie a thousand times, when it comes to me, I know she's telling the truth. Romeo looms behind her. I look away. Because I'm the liar by not telling her about Romeo.

I cast my gaze over the shallow end looking for my sister. Zora is always easy to find. But I don't see her. "Zora!" I shout. "Let's go." She doesn't answer. So I check the stairs, where I left her. She's not there. "Do you see Zora?"

Rose looks out at the water with me. I see lots of little white kid heads but no Zora head.

"What's wrong?" Ally says, pulling up beside us.

"Where's Zora? I can't find her."

"She's probably in the bathroom," Ally says. But I know she's not. Zora doesn't go to the pool bathroom without me.

That's when I start to freak out. "Zora!" I yell.

"Chill," Rose says, "we'll find her."

"Yeah, she's around." It's Romeo, coming to help.

We're searching the shallow end when I hear Mrs. Franklin's whistle break out in three urgent bursts. "Birdie, look!" Ally exclaims.

I turn to see Ally pointing. Toward the deep end. And then I see her. Zora. By herself. Standing at the top of the high dive.

"Zora!" I yell, and start running.

As Mrs. Franklin's whistle goes frantic, everyone clears out of the deep end. My sister stands absolutely frozen at the end of the high board. I don't take my eyes off her.

Zora is only seven. Truth be told, I didn't jump off the high dive until I was eight and it practically scared me to death. If Ally hadn't double dared me, I'm not sure I would have done it yet.

"Zora!" I call out. But she doesn't answer. Her terrified eyes are locked on the water below. "Zora, talk to me!"

Ally and Rose rush to my side. "Come on, Zora," Ally yells.

I know Zora better than anyone. So I know she's not moving. Once Zora freezes with fear, you practically need a blowtorch to thaw her out.

"Zora, come down off the board," Mrs. Franklin calls out over her loudspeaker. And I can feel Zora tense up even tighter. Giving Mrs. Franklin a pleading look, I hold up my hands to stop her from doing that again as I run to the high dive ladder.

It's twenty-two steps. I've counted them before. I count each one of them now, trying to calm myself down. As my head rises above the back of the diving board, I see her. "Zora, it's Birdie," I say softly. "I'm coming up."

Zora doesn't turn around. And I think, *How's she going to fly to Mars if she's scared of the high dive?* Maybe I'll have to go to Mars with her.

I step up onto the diving board. It's flat and solid, unlike the springboard below. As I walk out, holding on to the rail, I see every eye in the pool area watching us.

"I'm right behind you, Zora-pie," I say and keep walking. As I pass the end of the rail, I move across the open board, which hovers over the deep water.

"Got you." I grab her arm gently. "I got you. It's okay." But she doesn't move. She doesn't turn around. She's as still as a block of ice.

"Come on, Zora. Just turn around and I'll help you down."

"I can't." It comes out like a whimper.

"Yes, you can."

Ever so slightly, she shakes her head no.

"Just turn around. It's easy."

"No!" Zora whisper-yells.

I look down at my friends for help. "You should jump," Rose calls up. But gently. "You can do it. It's easy."

Zora grabs on to my arm for dear life but still doesn't turn from the spot. And I realize Rose is right. Jumping is the best way out of this.

"Let's jump, Zora," I say as brightly I can. "It'll be fun."

"No, Birdie." She's trembling now.

I lean down, my lips beside her ear, and whisper, "Why did you do this? Why did you come up here?"

It's very quiet before she says, "I wanted to fly."

I smile to myself. Of course she did. "So let's fly. We'll do it together."

"Nooooo!"

"Please," I say. "I'll let you play with Peg Leg for a whole week. You can sleep with him and everything."

Her head turns slightly. "Really?"

"Really. And it's no big deal. I'll stand right beside you. I'll hold your hand. We'll fly together."

"It's okay, Zora," yells Ally.

She shakes her head sharply. "I can't."

"Don't look down. Look up. Like the birds."

She squeezes my hand. I could jump off and pull her with me. It would work. It would get her down. But it also might scar her for life. And I would hate it if I was the reason she never went to Mars. Instead, I choose the greater good.

"We could turn around and climb down the ladder with everybody looking at us. Or they could all watch us jump. Think how jealous Rose and Ally will be." I feel her eyes shift to my friends by the side of the pool. "This will be just our thing. Only you and me, Zor." That last part was completely manipulative because I know Zora is sometimes jealous of my friends. But like I said, the greater good.

"Okay," Zora says quietly. "Okay."

I step beside her, locking eyes with Mrs. Franklin, who's probably going to put me in "tween time-out" for this because only one person is supposed to be on the high dive at a time. Not to mention if I had been watching her like I was supposed to, Zora wouldn't have climbed up here in the first place. But I can't think about that right now.

I take Zora's hand in mine and she looks up at me. "We're going to be birds," I say. "We're going to fly."

Her eyes turn forward like she's facing a firing squad.

"When I get to three. One . . . two . . . hold your breath, Zora . . . three."

And we fly.

25

THE LITTLE bell rings as I walk into the fabric store. I look at the shop, those four walls, with new eyes today. I can almost picture Smith and Sons.

Even though Ally and Rose want to be done with the mystery, done with the clues, I'm not. I've tried but I just can't help it. I opened Girl Detective's box. I was the one who found it. I was the one who dared. And now I can't let go. I need to know what happened. At this point, I'm not even sure why.

Going to the nursing home solved the mystery of Martin Smith but it did not solve the murders. I've spent days at the pool, trying to be normal again. Trying to do what my friends wanted. But last night, I couldn't help myself. I opened the clue box and reread the second clue, the one from the Gillans' mailbox.

Congratulations. You're smarter than you look.

Thank you very much, I thought.

Now you know. Again, I didn't know much.

Ruthie didn't go to see Gregg. That meant she didn't go see the Allman Brothers Band and that was established by the intact concert ticket. You're repeating yourself, G.D. The question now was why didn't Ruthie go to the concert and what happened instead?

Because of him. I guessed Martin Smith happened instead.

He knows how to use this. He was a butcher. And a murderer. Got it.

Of course he does! Got that, too.

Find him and you can find her. Ruthie? Her body? Her bones? Gross.

Keep following the clues! We found Smith and Sons. We found Henry Smith, but I don't feel any closer to finding the next clue.

But here's the Wrinkle—A wrinkle; an unexpected complication. Like I need that.

Then I read the last line. *Meg is waiting.* Meg. But who is Meg? And how do I find her?

It was Meg that sent me back to the fabric store. Meg made me lie to my dad and get him to drop me off at the library for an hour. "I'm old enough," I said. Even added, "Don't you trust me?"

He shouldn't. My awesome dad should not trust me. But he does. Even after telling him what happened with Zora at the pool, he does. And how do I repay his trust? After he dropped me off in front of the library, I watched him drive away, then crossed the street and headed directly for the fabric shop. I didn't even go inside the library. Instead, I walked into the fabric shop and stepped right up to the counter.

"Hi," Lucy says, recognizing me but not quite placing me.

"Hi. I'm Birdie from last week. My friend and I came in."

"Oh, yes. Birdie," Lucy says, the book of her mind flipping back to that page. "I remember. How can I help you? Not many girls your age want to sew these days."

Right, I'm in a fabric store, so I feel a little bad telling her that I'm not interested in sewing. As I look around the empty shop, I realize not many people in general are interested in sewing anymore. "I just have a question," I say to her. "It's about Meg."

I let the name sink in, studying her eyes for any sign of recognition.

"Meg who, dear?"

"Uh . . . that's what I was hoping you would know. She might have been a friend of Martin Smith's?" I look hopefully into her eyes but get back nothing. "She could have worked here? Maybe been his girlfriend?" I'm grasping because I really thought Lucy would know.

The blank expression on Lucy's face tells it all. "No, no Meg," she says. "None that I can remember."

Have I been totally wrong about everything? I was so sure the second clue was leading me to the butcher shop. But it's really been leading me to Meg. If Lucy doesn't know who Meg is, how am I supposed to find out?

For the first time, it feels like I've reached a real and true dead end—the wall at end of the road. I lean my face against the cold, hard brick and think, *If Meg is waiting for me, she might be waiting forever.*

"Are you all right, dear?" Lucy asks.

I nod, say a quiet yes, and slip out of the shop without another word.

At the library, I stare at the same page of the same book for the next forty-five minutes. My mind is racing, going around the same track over and over again. At full speed and getting nowhere.

The big clock on the wall says my dad will be back any minute. I take the book to the checkout and hand Mrs. Thompson my library card.

"Hi, Birdie," she says and steps off her perch. She scans my card and punches the keyboard, waking her computer. "I've still saved those books in the back for you if you're interested."

Oh no. Mrs. Thompson, the greatest librarian in the world, saved me books, and in my hunt for Martin Smith, I forgot all about it. "I'm really sorry," I say. "I had to leave early last time. I should have told you."

"It's okay. Stuff happens. Give me a sec." She walks into the room behind the counter while I stand there staring at the wall. In less than a minute, she's back, books in hand. "I'm an expert at hiding the good stuff," she says with a wink.

I smile a thank-you. Not my usual library smile, a half-hearted one.

"You coming to see her?" she asks, turning to the poster behind the counter. I didn't even realize I had been staring at it.

"Ms. McAllister is going to read from her new book before the signing. She writes adult fiction. Actually, she writes murder mysteries, so I wouldn't recommend her to most young readers but I think you can handle it."

I look at the picture of Emily McAllister. "Dad said she's big-time."

"Very big-time," Mrs. Thompson says and hands me my books.

"So why is she coming here?"

"Read, Birdie." She points to the poster where it says *Atlanta native*. "She grew up in Atlanta."

"That's cool," I say.

"Yes. Very cool, indeed."

26

"**RUTHIE DELGADO** is alive."

I must look like I've swallowed a fly or something, because Rose leads me to the clubhouse steps and sits me in the shade. "Breathe, Bird," she says.

"What did you say?" I ask.

"Breathe."

"No, about Ruthie."

"She's alive," Rose says. "Ruthie D. is in the land of the living."

"How do you know?"

"Easy. I looked for her where all old people end up," she says. "Facebook."

I gaze up at Rose and feel a little queasy and don't know why. Ruthie Delgado is alive. That's good news. That's what we wanted. So why am I suddenly feeling carsick and no one's stopping the car?

Ally walks toward us, dripping from the pool. "What are you talking about?"

"You!" Rose says. But I miss the beat. My *you* comes out as an afterthought.

"What's wrong?" Ally asks me.

"Nothing." I look up, squinting against the sun. "Ruthie's alive."

"Huh? I thought we weren't doing that anymore."

"We weren't," Rose says and sits beside me on the stairs. "But then I woke up this morning with this Facebook idea. My mum Facebooks her friends back in England all the time. They're all on Facebook. And since I'd already decrypted her password, you know, it was easy. I just looked her up."

"Why didn't we think of this sooner?" I ask, truly dumbfounded by the oversight.

"I don't know. We must be idiots. Anyway," Rose continues, "she lives in Michigan now. Her last name is Bayer."

"But how do you know it's really her?" I ask.

"A couple of reasons. One, old people don't know how to leave their year of birth off Facebook, and Ruthie Delgado Bayer is no exception. Year of birth: 1957. Check. Also, she went to Crestwood High School."

We stare at her blankly. "So?" Ally asks.

"So," Rose replies. "I did some research. Crestwood High School opened in 1971. Right in time for Ruthie Delgado to go to school there. And it closed in 1992 to become a middle school. So Crestwood High School became . . ." She looks at us like we're supposed to know the answer and then gives up. "Monarch Middle School."

"The old middle school?" I ask.

"Yep."

"So I'll be going to what used to be Ruthie Delgado's high school?" Ally asks.

"Exactly."

I lean back on the stairs and take this in. Frankly, I can't help but feel a little inferior. Why didn't I think of looking on Facebook? Why didn't I find out about Crestwood High School? "You're a regular Sherlock Holmes this morning, Rose," I say, trying to hide my jealousy. "What's gotten into you?"

"Don't know. Maybe cuz of all this extra time not playing violin. And look!" She holds out the fingertips of her left hand. "Hardly any calluses anymore."

She can believe it if it makes her feel better, but it's been less than a week, so those calluses aren't fading yet. What *is* fading is our summer, which is ticking down like a time bomb.

And now Ruthie is alive.

"Oh, and that's not everything," Rose states triumphantly. "I found her number, too. That was easy once I knew where she lived. So what do you say? Let's give Ruthie a call."

"Hello."

The voice answers on the second ring. We're in Rose's bedroom, having threaded our way through unpacked boxes and screeching packing tape.

"Hello," I say into Rose's phone, my eyes widening. "Is this Ruthie Delgado?"

"This is Ruth Bayer," the not-so-friendly voice answers. "Who is this?"

"Um." I look to Rose and Ally. "Well, I'm calling from Atlanta. My name is Birdie Adams. I think you used to live next door to where I live now."

"On Gainsborough?"

"Yes, on Gainsborough!" I say excitedly. This is her. This is our Ruthie. "So you're really alive?"

"What?" she says. It's only one word but it's a suspicious one.

"Oh, I mean, well, we found this ticket to the Allman Brothers Band concert and it was yours and the person who buried it thought you were dead. And I mean, we've been trying to solve the mystery. To find out if Martin Smith really killed you. Because Girl Detective was really convinced that he did, but if you're alive then—"

"Who is this again?"

I hold the phone away from my face and look pleadingly at Rose, who mouths, *She thinks you're crazy.*

"Oh, I'm not crazy or anything," I say back into the phone. But as soon as I say it, I realize that makes me sound even crazier.

"Right," Ruthie says. "Whatever kind of crank call this is, I'm not interested. Especially if you know Martin Smith. Call me again and I'll call the police."

"But—"

The phone goes dead in my hand. I hold it out to Rose as if she can give it mouth-to-mouth resuscitation and bring Ruthie back.

"Way to play it cool, Bird," she says, taking the phone from my hand.

"Yeah, way to scare the crap out of her," says Ally.

"You think I scared her?"

"Just a little," Rose answers, and starts to laugh.

"Oh no!" I put my hands over my eyes. What is wrong with me?!

"Yeah, but she's alive," Ally says. "That was really her, right?"

"Yeah, it was. She said Gainsborough Drive. And she knew who Martin Smith was. So we were right about him, too."

"Except for the part about him killing her. But who cares?!" Rose declares and throws her hands up. "Mystery solved! The Case of the Buried Box is finally finished."

"Well, kind of."

"Birdie!" they both exclaim.

"Okay, okay. Mystery solved," I say. Except no matter what they say, it's not. Because what about Girl Detective? We still don't know what happened to her.

After eating sandwiches that Mrs. Ashcroft made us for lunch, we start back outside to go to our island, when Rose's mom says, "Why don't you and Ally nip back to the pool, Rose. I'd like to have a word with Birdie."

Rose and my eyes meet. "Mum!" she says.

"Shan't be for long. Now, off you pop." As Rose's mom shoos them out the front door, I catch one last look at Rose's pleading eyes before the front door closes.

When Rose's mom returns, she asks me to sit down again. And I do. I sit at the kitchen table and do my best to act like everything is normal.

Instead of joining me, she glowers over me like Professor McGonagall. "So, Birdie. What do you know about Rose's violin?"

I force my eyes to meet hers. If I look away, she'll know I'm hiding something.

"Well," I start to say, and thankfully, the kettle blows and she walks to the counter to turn it off. She places two tea bags into a teapot and fills the pot with boiling water. I've seen her do this hundreds of times.

As the tea brews, she sits down in the chair across from me. There might as well be a single lightbulb strung over my head. I steel for the interrogation.

"I can't imagine someone coming into our house and stealing Rose's violin. I'm not buying it." She watches me closely. "I thought you might have something to add to the story."

I shrug. I really don't want to lie to her. How did I get to the point where I feel like I need to lie to so many adults? "Not really," I say.

"You have nothing to say?"

"I just know what Rose told me." Yeah, that's a lie. Could I possibly consider this a lie for the greater good? It's for my greater good, for sure. Rose would be so upset if I told her mom the truth. But is it for the real greater good? "I really loved listening to Rose play violin," I tell her. Because that is true. "But maybe it'll be good for her to have a break. I think she was starting to . . . I don't know . . . resent it."

"Hmm." Her eyes are working hard, trying to crack me open, to see what's inside. "It's a sin to waste a talent," she finally says. "Rose needs to play. She needs to practice."

"Maybe when she gets back to England," I say and feel my eyes unexpectedly fill. I drop my head and just sit there silently, waiting for more questions, wiping my eyes with the back of my hand. Instead, Rose's mom pats my hand with hers. "You've been a good friend, Birdie. Rose is lucky to have you."

27

THE LAST place I expected to end up today was in Joey Wachowski's TV room. But here I am. Here we are. And it's practically a miracle.

When I got to the island, after my talk with Rose's mom, Rose jumped up as soon as she saw me and asked, "What did she say?"

"Nothing, really. She just asked me about the violin."

"And?"

"I was cool."

Rose let out a sigh of relief and sat back down under the willow tree. I plopped down, completing the circle between her and Ally, our cross-legged knees touching. There was a weird feeling in my stomach. I wondered if, in a year from now, our circle would be unbroken? Would being a good friend to Rose really mean anything then?

We'd been sitting for all of two minutes when a voice made us jump back to our feet. It was Romeo, boarding our island and yelling for us.

Out of breath, he exclaimed, "There you are!" He wasn't looking at Rose and he wasn't looking at me. He was looking at Ally. "I've been searching for you everywhere!"

"He fell off the rope swing too close to the edge," Romeo whispers. "Hit a rock. And *crack*."

"We heard it and everything," Connor says, making a weird bone-crunching sound.

There's a rope swing upstream from our island where the boys hang out. It's up a steep cliff and it's dangerous and some boys are dumb.

We got to Joey's house by bike caravan and Romeo wouldn't tell us anything along the way. He and Connor led us into Joey's TV room, where the big boy was draped across the sofa like a fallen soldier. With a cast on his right arm.

"I can't believe you fell off the rope swing," says Rose. "You really are the complete package. Charm *and* grace."

"Shhhh!" Joey puts his left index finger to his lips. "My mom would crap if she knew I did this on the rope swing." As one, our eyes shift toward the kitchen, where Joey's mom is wiping the counter, and we become suspiciously silent.

"Everything okay in there?" Joey's mom calls out.

"Yes," Joey calls back. "We're fine. Thanks for asking, Mom."

Rose's face scrunches. "What excellent manners, Joseph. So refreshing and unexpected."

He rolls his eyes. "Shut up, string bean," he says, like himself again, but quietly, so his mom won't hear.

"What are you going to do?" Ally asks. She's staring at the cast on Joey's arm with real and true concern. "The game's this Saturday!"

"Well, yeah," Joey says, his chest deflating.

"Yeah," Romeo says. "That's why we asked you here." Romeo nudges Joey.

"Do I have to?"

Romeo's hands fly up, his face ready to explode. "Really? Come on, Joe."

Joey glances down at the cast on his arm, then turns to Ally. "As you can see, this really sucks."

"Totally sucks," Ally says. "I hate the Broncos, but I hate the Condors more. Who's going to pitch if you don't? You guys have got to win."

"We thought you'd see it that way," Romeo says.

"That's really tough luck," Ally adds earnestly.

I look at Romeo. Is he hiding a grin?

"So, Blondie, that's why we called you here," Joey says. "We talked to Coach and the whole team agrees. If we're going to win, we need a good pitcher." Romeo pokes his leg. "Okay, a *great* pitcher. And if yours truly is not available, then there's no other choice. We need you, Blondie. We need you to pitch the game on Saturday."

"Huh?" Ally says, stunned.

"Yeah, can you do it? I mean it'll be a great opportunity for you, too. It's not all about the Broncos."

"But mostly about the Broncos," Rose says and elbows Ally back to life.

"Yeah," says Ally breathlessly. "Of course—"

"Wait!" I hold up my hands. "There's a condition."

"What?" Joey says. "No conditions!"

"Only one, Joey. But it's a deal breaker."

Ally turns to me. She's afraid I'm going to ruin this. I can see it in her eyes. But I'm not. I've got this.

Joey groans. "What is it?"

"Ask her again," I say.

"Huh?"

"Just ask her again. The right way."

Joey shoots me a look, then says, "Okay, Blondie, will you—"

I clear my throat pointedly. The confused look on Joey's face tells me volumes about his intellectual capacity. Romeo leans over and whispers in his ear. "Oh," Joey says, finally getting it. "Do I have to?"

"I'm going to throw you off that swing myself!" Romeo exclaims, but softly, keeping an eye on the kitchen and Joey's mom. "Dude!"

"Okay, okay." Joey looks at Ally. "Blon—I mean . . . Ally—will you pitch for me in the game on Saturday? Please?"

A smile blossoms across Ally's face, but she buries it quickly and gives Joey a shrug. "Yeah, I guess."

"You guess?" I say. "Are you kidding?"

Her smile returns like the sun. "Yeah, I'm kidding! Heck, yeah, I'll pitch for you, Joey! I can't wait to be a Bronco!"

28

I'M IN the library the day before the big charity game, flipping through *James and the Giant Peach*. The oldest copy they have. It's been read hundreds of times—you can tell by the worn pages.

I remember thinking how unbelievable it was when the peach rolled over Aunt Sponge and Aunt Spiker and flattened them into human pancakes. And how cool it was when the peach floated out to sea and ended up on the Empire State Building.

If I had a giant peach, maybe it could take Ally and me to England to visit Rose. Ha. Rose would freak out if the giant peach rolled up in front of her house and Ally and me got out. Especially if we brought along Miss Spider and the Old-Green-Grasshopper.

Rose is packing and Ally is practicing. Dad took Zora to play miniature golf. He's trusting me again to be alone at the library and this time he can. I sit at a cubicle near the front. Out the window, I can see the fabric store. No need to go there today. No need to go there ever again. Meg was never at the fabric shop. Lucy doesn't know a Meg and neither do I. Girl Detective's Meg might as well be a ghost.

I feel like being alone today. I watch big white cumulus clouds roll in and think about Ally. She's been practicing with the Broncos since Joey asked her to pitch for him. She's getting a second chance, and even her brother Mark is helping her get ready.

Ally is getting what she wants.

Rose is getting what she wants, too. In a way. She has liberated herself from her violin. I think about that poor, burned-out violin lying abandoned somewhere in our creek. And although Mrs. Ashcroft has assured her there will be a new violin once they get to London, for now Rose is free. At least for a little while longer.

So I'm left wondering—what do I want?

The summer is almost over and what have I done? I've followed these crazy clues to nowhere. Yeah, it was exciting to find the clue box on the island. It was pretty amazing that the knife was actually hidden under the bird in the Gillans' mailbox. And I found them. I did that.

But since then, it's been a giant waste of summer. My detecting skills have failed me completely. Sneaking over to the fabric store. Taking the bus trip to Decatur. We could have been swimming. We could have been hanging out. Soon we'll be heading to Chicago to visit Grandma before school starts. And Rose will be gone for good.

I close *James and the Giant Peach* and carry it back to the shelf. The fabric shop was a dead end. I see that so clearly now. But I can't help thinking about Meg. It's not a common name. I don't know any Megs. I've never met anybody named that.

I slip *James* back in its place on the shelf and lean against the Roald Dahl section feeling defeated. I've spent so much time wandering this long row of books. Most of them I have read. They can whisper to me because I know their secrets.

I stand there staring at nothing. Just the *L*s, those books across from me whose authors' names begin with the letter *L*. I'm about to walk away, when I realize what I am looking at.

Her.

My mouth falls open. Because, of course, I know a Meg. I've known a Meg for years. She's one of my favorite people. But this Meg?

I pull out a copy of *A Wrinkle in Time* from the shelf across from me. In it, Meg Murry goes on a journey through time and space to rescue her father. Like me, she has a scientist mother. Like me, she feels different from the rest of her family. Like me, she is dealt an incredible mystery to solve over one stormy summer.

I look at the cover—the one with the centaur—and remember the clue and the words I didn't understand: *But here's the Wrinkle.* That was what Girl Detective wrote right before *Meg is waiting*.

When I read it before, I had thought it meant there'd be a complication. A wrinkle. I had noticed she capitalized the *W* but I didn't think it meant anything. But it did. Because *Wrinkle* is part of the name of a book that happens to be about a girl named Meg.

I gaze at the book and wonder. What if she wasn't sending me to the fabric store? What if she's been sending me to the library all along?

To Meg.

It hits me like a wave.

Sweeping all six copies of *A Wrinkle in Time* from the shelf, I rush them to a nearby table and lay them before me. Three have the Centaur cover, two show the night sky surrounded by book images, and the last one is a picture of a dove sitting atop an egg filled with three children.

A Wrinkle in Time is old. Flipping to the copyright page, I see it was first published in 1963.

The timeline works.

One by one, I strum through the pages of each book, searching for a clue. But nothing. Then I realize why. None of these editions is old enough. These books were published after Girl Detective was here.

Even if I'm right and Meg Murry is the Meg I'm looking for, the *A Wrinkle in Time* that Girl Detective entrusted with her next clue is long gone—lost or recycled in the forgotten dump heap of old library books. My heart sinks. Too late. I'm too late.

Closing my eyes, I search for Girl Detective through time and space. I see her blue eyes. The ones from the bottom of the creek. And tell her I'm sorry.

With a tip of my finger, I shut the cover of the last book

before me. It falls onto its pages like a freshly cut tree collapsing onto a leafy forest floor. It's finally time to close the book on Girl Detective. To close the book on all of it.

After returning all the *Wrinkle*s back to the shelf, I pick up *James and the Giant Peach* again. It feels like comfort food in my hand as I carry it to the checkout counter.

"Get everything you need?" Mrs. Thompson asks.

"Not really," I say.

Mrs. Thompson stops mid-scan. "What's the matter? You never look like this when you're checking out a book."

I force a smile. "I'm fine." But I'm not fine. A part of me wants to tell Mrs. Thompson all about it. How I can't find Girl Detective because I was born too late.

"Okay, but I've seen that troubled look before," she says. "At some point, you'll need to unload it."

I nod and take *James* in my arms. "Thanks," I say and start to turn but don't. I look up at the librarian. "Mrs. Thompson?"

She peers over her computer. "Yes, Birdie."

"What happens to old books that the library doesn't want anymore?"

"What do you mean?"

"You know, the old ones. The special ones that got too old or too fragile to stay. What happens to them?"

Mrs. Thompson grins oddly. "Oh, dear." She glances over her shoulder, then leans in conspiratorially. "We do have a little secret."

29

I CAN'T believe it. I cannot believe what I am seeing.

This is not my library. It can't be. This is like some secret hidden chamber from an old Nancy Drew mystery. But here it is. We walked through the door behind the checkout counter, the door I've seen hundreds of times, and it's like we've stepped into another world. I'm standing in the middle of it, astounded. Gazing at all the books. Stacks and shelves of them.

"This used to be the whole library," Mrs. Thompson says from beside me. "It was like this when it was first built. Wasn't very much back then."

"But it's beautiful," I say, staring at the wooden walls and the beams that reach to the ceiling. As I look up, a "wow" escapes my lips.

"Isn't it amazing?" Mrs. Thompson says.

"Yeah," I answer, our heads tilting upward. There's a huge painting up there. Right on the ceiling. And even though the room isn't especially large, the mural is. It dominates, with its white clouds and green countryside. Its old-timey train station. The horse-drawn wagon. The man with the reins in his hands. The girl with the red hair sitting beside him. "Is that Anne Shirley?" I ask.

"Yes, it is." I can tell she's proud of me for knowing that. "*Anne of Green Gables* was still a big deal when this library was built." She pauses. "For some of us, it's still a big deal."

"Who painted it?"

"I don't even know. Mrs. Parsons could tell us if she were still alive. She was the librarian back then. For years and years and years. I remember her from when I was a girl. Children were afraid of her because her mouth turned down in a rather permanent frown. But she wasn't mean. She loved books. And she loved readers. She showed me this room when I was about your age." She turns to me and smiles. "There weren't as many books in here then."

I peel my eyes from the ceiling and let them linger over all the volumes—old books on shelves and piled in tall stacks all around us.

"As a librarian, we're trained to cull the old books that are too delicate for general usage. But Mrs. Parsons had a hard time with that. She gave away hundreds of old books but there were some she couldn't part with. Ms. Lincoln, the librarian after Mrs. Parsons, kept up the tradition. And then there was me."

"These are the old books?"

"Not all of them, of course. This room would be bursting twenty times over if we kept everything. Just certain ones."

"I'm looking for *A Wrinkle in Time*," I say resolutely. "An early one."

"An early one," Mrs. Thompson says, thinking. "That was before my time here but . . . maybe . . . why don't you look over there?" She points to the corner of the room, at a spot under the old-timey train on the ceiling.

The buzzer rings. "That's for me," she says.

"This is where the buzzer goes?"

"This is where the buzzer goes." She grins. "Now, go find your book."

As she leaves the room, I make my way through the maze of books to the corner under Anne Shirley's train. There are so many books here. I search up and down the stacks, recognizing some but not many.

After having no luck in several stacks, my eyes shift to the shelves. There are mostly kids' books in this corner but there are some adult ones, too. And forget about anything called alphabetical order.

I'm never going to find it, I think as my eyes get lost in the titles and authors. And how do I even know this is one of the books Mrs. Parsons or Ms. Lincoln saved? I'm searching for the long shot of long shots.

Instead of bending down to the bottom shelves, I sit on the floor so I can more easily see the low ones. I lean in close and examine title after title. After title. To the end of the row.

Nothing.

No *A Wrinkle in Time.*

No Meg.

Hmmmm. I stare at the ceiling, at Anne Shirley, heading to her new life at Green Gables. Things must have been so much simpler back then. Turning, I lean forward to stand—

and stop cold. Between *The Wonderful Wizard of Oz* and *The Wind in the Willows,* in the stack I haven't searched yet, I see it.

A Wrinkle in Time. By Madeleine L'Engle.

Waiting patiently for me.

I begin unstacking like mad. The first handful of books goes on one stack. The next handful onto another. Until I'm staring down at a blue dust jacket with white words written on it that say: *A Wrinkle in Time,* next to three white silhouette figures surrounded with circles. I recognize these fictional figures to be Charles Wallace Murry, Calvin O'Keefe, and Meg Murry. My Meg.

I lift the book like it is a sacred tome and it falls open in my hand. The pages are yellowed, some of them torn. I rest it on top of a book stack and carefully turn the pages. When I reach the end, there is a sinking feeling in my stomach. Because nothing's there.

Looking up at Anne, I whisper, "Little help, please." But Anne has very little to contribute, so I turn back to the book in my hand. I hold it up and inspect it from all angles. I open it again and examine the inside of the front cover. Then, I search the inside of the back cover.

The stamped checkout card is there. Mrs. Thompson told me that before the computer checkout system, library books used to be checked out using a card that lived in a little pocket on the inside back cover of a book. The card was stamped with the date the book was due back so it became a record of when a book was taken from the library.

I pull the card out of the card slot and scan down, looking

at the dates until I get to the last stamp: JAN 3 '74. That must have been the last time the book was checked out before it was pulled from circulation and ended up here.

Scanning up the card, I stop at JUN 24 '73. That would be about the right time. Soon after the Allman Brothers Band concert. Soon after Ruthie didn't show up at the Omni Coliseum.

Girl Detective was here. I can feel it. I find myself inspecting the front cover again and realize something isn't quite right. The inside paper lining appears somehow wrong. Like someone carefully glued in a piece of blue card stock to make it look like the real inside cover when it really wasn't. But why would somebody do a thing like that?

With my fingernail, I scratch at the top corner of the blue card stock. Because there's only one reason someone would do that. To hide something.

Once I get it started, the fake panel begins to peel away easily. Slowly, what's hiding behind it is revealed.

A photograph. An old black-and-white one. Not a Polaroid but a real picture about the size of a 4×6, but not exactly. Gently, I lift it from its hiding place.

It's a picture of a rather large brick house with a chimney and wooden shutters. The lawn in front is mostly bare with only a couple of small trees.

I flip the photo over, and written on the back in blue ink is the next clue:

Good work, detective.
You're almost home.

The evidence you need
Lives where I used to
Upstairs. Second on right,
Creaky floorboard by the bookshelf.
Thank you.

Holy smokes! This is where she lived. This is Girl Detective's house. Find the house and I find her.

And just like that, in the middle of this insane room with all these books, I know what I want. I want to finish the mystery. I want to meet Girl Detective, dead or alive, and find out what happened. I want to know why she asked me to Open If You Dare. And why she led me to find dead Martin and alive Ruthie.

I want to know what it's all been for.

While slipping the old picture inside my copy of *James and the Giant Peach*, I whisper a small good-bye to Anne Shirley. As I turn to go, I hear the words form in my head:

Girl Detective, I'm coming for you.

PART 5

A DARK AND STORMY NIGHT

30

"STRIKE THREE!" the umpire calls out and everyone in our bleachers cheers. That's where Rose and I are sitting watching Ally strike out another Condor.

"Way to go, Ally!" Joey calls from the dugout. It's already the sixth inning and the Broncos are leading 2–0. The sun is blazing and I don't know how Ally's doing it. When I called her last night, she said she'd had a stomachache all day. And this morning, when Rose and I met her at the concession stand before the game, she still wasn't feeling so great. But there she is, like some kind of mythical warrior, battling the Condors *and* the midday sun.

We're at the big baseball field at our park—the one with the tallest bleachers, the biggest scoreboard, and the most official announcer. Broncos fans crowd the bleachers on the third-base side, Condors on the first-base side. On the field, Romeo's behind Ally at third base and Connor's at first. They've got her back today.

The General, Mark, Zora, and my parents sit on the row behind us. Simon and Ashley are a few bleachers up.

I'm wearing a white shirt and rainbow shorts, and Rose is in her yellow overall shorts and a tee. It's so hot, I feel like my sweat is sweating. Rose leans into me and whispers, "This is my last baseball game. Maybe ever."

I hate to be reminded of that. There are so many lasts this summer and they're tumbling over like dominoes. And my mom has already started packing us for Chicago.

Another batter walks up to the plate. "Come on, Ally," my dad calls out. Her eyes peek our way before turning back to business. She pulls down the front of her Broncos hat, winds up, and throws. Whoa.

"Strike!"

"She's doing so great, Jill," my mom says to the General.

The General puts her finger to her lips. "Let's not jinx it."

My mom gives me the look. The one that says there is no scientific basis for "jinxing" things and I'm not to believe such nonsense. Honestly, I'm not sure which mother is actually right.

"Strike two!"

My eyes wander to the announcer's booth. We saw the middle school coach go up there at the start of the game. He's been watching Ally this whole time. I wonder what Joey thinks of this. Ally doing this great in front of Coach Rodriguez might change his chances in the coming year with the old middle school team. He's being pretty cool, though. For Joey.

Crack. The batter makes contact and hits the ball hard. "Line drive," the announcer cries. Everyone stands as a collective "ooh" erupts from our bleachers. Romeo dives and makes the catch. The ump calls the out and the announcer shouts, "What a catch by third baseman, Romeo Dawson!"

"Yay, Romeo!" Rose yells, and claps. I clap, too. It was pretty incredible.

The next batter approaches the plate. One more out and the inning is over. One more inning and Ally has won the game. Ally throws and, "Strike!" It's all going her way. Until Rose elbows me in the arm—hard.

"What?!" I turn, ready to elbow her back. But Rose is not looking at me. She's staring at Ally, in a very weird way.

"Look," she whispers. "When she throws."

I watch as Ally pitches but don't see anything. The umpire calls a ball and our entire bleachers boo him. Except for Rose. She can't keep her eyes off Ally.

"Maybe I'm seeing things," she whispers again. "I hope I'm seeing things. Just look. When she steps forward. Look at the inside of her pants."

Ally winds up and throws, her left leg coming forward off the mound as she releases her fast ball.

"Oh no," I say quietly, and squeeze Rose's knee. Whipping around, I wave the General toward me. She leans down and I whisper in her ear, "Ally's got her period!"

The General's eyes seek out the red spot of blood trickling down the inside of Ally's white baseball pant leg. "Oh no," she echoes, and grabs my shoulder. "As soon as she gets off the field, you girls get her to the bathroom." She doesn't wait for a response.

"Where's she going? What's wrong?" Mom asks, and I whisper what's happened in her ear.

As soon as we hear "Strike three!" from the field, my mom says, "Come on." The inning ends and the players are leaving the field. We pass Mark on the way to the stairs.

"What's up?" he calls out.

"Later!" Rose answers as Ally sees us heading her way.

I close the door to the bathroom with a loud clunk and lock it.

"What's up?" Ally cries. "I can't be goofing around!"

"We're not goofing," Rose says.

"We're not, Al," I say, shaking my head and looking down at her pants.

"What are you looking at?" Ally asks and looks, too. Like it's no big deal. Until it's a humongous deal. "OH MY GOD!" she cries. "WHAT'S HAPPENING?"

"It's okay, it's okay," I say, trying to calm her.

"It's your period," Rose tells her.

"My period?" she says in total disbelief, even though we learned all about it when they gave us the talk in school last year. "But I'm only eleven."

"I know. But—"

"I can't have my period today! I've got to finish the game!" Ally grabs my arm like a lifeline. "Did anybody see it? Do the boys know?"

"I don't think so." I look to Rose.

"Nah. Boys are too dumb to notice something like that. We caught it in time."

"You sure?"

"Absolutely," Rose says and I nod, having no idea whether they saw it or not.

There's a knock on the door and Ally freezes like it's the police.

"It's your mom." I open the door, and the General and my mom slip inside.

The General drops a backpack on the floor and starts unzipping it. "I was afraid something like this might happen," she says. "But why today?" She pulls out a pair of underwear, blue jeans, and a box of maxi pads and hands them to my mom.

"What is this?" Ally asks, her eyes bugging out.

"I got my period when I was eleven," the General says. "Before all of my older friends. Happened at school and I didn't know what was going on. I know we've talked about it, but we probably should have talked more. I packed a bag and hid it in the car, just in case. But I really didn't think it would happen so soon."

Dumbstruck, Ally stares at her mom.

"Are you okay, sweetie?" the General asks in the gentlest tone I have ever heard come out of her mouth.

"Yeah," Ally croaks quietly.

"Okay." The General turns toward us. "Give us a few minutes. Okay?"

"Yes," my mom answers. "Let's go, girls. Mrs. Lorenz has got this."

The bathroom door closes behind us, and my mom, Rose, and I stand awkwardly outside.

"Wow," Rose finally says.

"It's going to be all right," says my mom.

"Yeah, but why did it have to happen today?" I ask. Mom puts her arm around me and pulls us out of the sun. I look up at her. "When is it going to happen to us?"

"Sooner than I'm ready."

I remember Ally's phone call from the night before and say, "So that's why Ally wasn't feeling good."

"Yeah," Rose says.

"Sometimes it doesn't make you feel good," Mom says. "But it's part of becoming a woman and all that. Biological. Scientifically sound." She gives us a motherly look. "It'll be okay. I didn't have mine until thirteen, so you probably have a little time. We'll get prepared." She looks at Rose. "You should ask your mom about it. So you can be ready, too."

Rose nods but I can tell she's a little freaked-out inside.

The bathroom door opens slightly. "Glad you're still here." The General leans through the crack. "Birdie, we need you."

I slip into the bathroom and look at Ally, who's standing in her Broncos shirt and new underwear. "What's up?"

"She can't pitch in jeans. It's too hot. And that's all we've got," the General says, eyeballing my rainbow shorts.

"Oh." I look down at my shorts. "Oh!"

By the time we're walking back to the bleachers, me wearing Ally's jeans on the hottest day of the year, the Broncos coach is going nuts. Joey runs up to us and yells, "Where's Blond—I mean Ally?!"

"She's coming," my mom answers. "Slight wardrobe malfunction. That's all."

"Yeah, cool your jets," says Rose.

"Here she comes," I say as Ally and her mom turn the corner heading our way.

The General marches over to the agitated coach, and I hear her say, "Her pants ripped." A real and true Greater-Good lie. Way to go, Gen.

Ally grabs her glove from the dugout and heads back toward the pitcher's mound, my rainbow shorts hanging out from under her Broncos jersey. There are murmurs all around, especially from the other players.

"What's with the shorts, Al?" Romeo calls out from third base.

"It's too hot out here," she answers, all relaxed-like. "Needed to cool down."

And just like that, Ally settles in.

She strikes out every Condor who comes to the plate.

She wins the inning. And wins the game.

After the ball game, the boys, led by Joey, lift Ally up on their shoulders and everything. Riding high, she throws off her hat and pulls the tie out of her hair. With her long blond hair flowing, there is no doubt that a girl just won the big game.

31

THE PLAN had been to go swimming after the game, and the boys wanted us to come, but it starts to look like rain. And with Ally's new development, we decide to hang out at my house. The General drops her off after being sure Ally wasn't too traumatized.

"It's like a mouse mattress. No joke," Ally says, adjusting how she sits on my bed. "Weird, you know."

"No, I don't," Rose says.

"I'm just glad it happened at the end of the game, not the beginning," Ally says. "Pitching seven innings with this thing between my legs would have been murder!"

"TMI, Al!" Rose exclaims.

"No such thing as TMI on this topic," I say. "This is real girl stuff that we've got to share. Let's commemorate." I pick up my Polaroid camera.

"What? Getting my period or winning the game?"

"Both," I say and squeeze in between Rose and Ally on the bed. "Smile." Instead, we make funny faces as I click the button. As soon as the undeveloped photo shoots out of the camera, Rose pulls it off and starts blowing on it.

"Why are you doing that?" I ask.

"On the Internet, it says if you blow on a Polaroid picture, it develops faster."

"Is that where you learn everything?" I ask.

Rose nods. "Pretty much."

"Does this mean I'm more mature than you guys?" Ally asks, her face absolutely serious. "Now, I mean?"

Rose and I look at each other and bust up laughing. "No!" I say.

"Absolutely not!" declares Rose.

Ally's face falls. "Oh. I just thought . . ."

"You're definitely more mature than yesterday," I say because she suddenly looks so sad.

"Oh, good." And Ally's smiling again, her mood changing at the rate of a golden retriever's.

"Speaking of pictures . . ." I grab my library copy of *James and the Giant Peach* and pull out the photo I found yesterday in *A Wrinkle in Time*. I told them about my whole adventure before the game but they have yet to see the actual picture of the house. "What do you think?" I hold up the black-and-white photo and watch them study it.

"It's a house," Rose says.

"An old one," adds Ally.

"It's the house where Girl Detective lived."

They examine it more closely. "Have you ever seen that house before?" Ally asks me.

"Maybe," I say, unconvincingly.

"You know it could be anywhere," Rose says and flips onto her back, looking up at the ceiling.

"Yeah, but it could be around here," I say. "Why would she bury the box on our island if she didn't live in our neighborhood?"

"Good point," Ally says.

"And I feel like the final clue is just waiting for us under a creaky floorboard by a bookshelf in her bedroom. Just like the clue said. Rose, look at it again." I hand her the picture. "If this is what Girl Detective's house looked like back then, what do you think it looks like now?"

Rose gives it serious attention, then hands the photo back to me. "Old."

I gaze down at the black-and-white image in my hand and silently agree. It would definitely look old by now.

"Popcorn!" My mom's voice calls up from downstairs. "And Zora's putting on a movie. You girls want to come watch?"

None of us moves until we hear a burst of thunder and Rose says, "I'll go."

"It's not even raining yet!" I say.

"It's not the rain I'm scared of," she says and heads toward the stairs.

"Chicken," Ally jokes and pulls a book from my shelf. She plops back on my bed. "I want popcorn!"

"She's not coming back," I say.

"And I'm not watching *Frozen*."

I look down on my bedspread and see that our Polaroid

selfie has developed nicely. Rose is doing moose ears with her hands, Ally is sticking out her tongue, and I've got my eyes crossed. I take the picture to my corkboard and pin it to an open spot near the center. Only a few more selfies and my corkboard will be completely full.

"What's this?"

"What's what?" I ask.

"This," Ally says and I turn around. She's sitting up, holding my copy of *When You Reach Me* in one hand and a little card in the other. A Valentine's card.

"No, give me that!" I rush over but Ally springs to the other side of the bed, putting the mattress between us.

She reads from the card: *"Roses are red, Violets are blue, Didn't want a girlfriend, Until I met you."*

"Come on, Al."

"Romeo likes you?!"

"Not so loud." I stare at her, wishing desperately that I had destroyed Romeo's card on the day I got it. "Yeah," I finally say. "He does."

"Since Valentine's Day and you never told me!"

It thunders loudly and I close the bedroom door. "How could I? If I told you, you'd say we have to tell Rose and—"

"We have to tell Rose."

"We can't tell her. She'll hate me."

"Do you like him back?" Ally asks.

"I don't know. No! He's a nice guy but I don't want a boyfriend." I look at the book that was supposed to guard my secret and want to strangle it. "Ugh! Since when do you read?"

"Funny."

"She's going to feel like an idiot. I've let her make a fool of herself with Romeo when I knew he didn't like her."

"Yeah, you did."

"But I didn't want to hurt her," I say. "You get that, right? You know, for the greater good."

Ally shakes her head. "Doesn't matter. There's no greater good with us."

I sit beside her on the bed. I know she's right but . . . "She's moving, Al. In a couple of weeks. Maybe she never has to find out. Maybe we can just let it go."

"Let it go, let it go," she sings, like Elsa from *Frozen*. Then looks at me. "No."

"Why?"

"Because we're friends! We don't keep secrets. Not from each other."

I trace the line of a big purple bedspread-flower with my finger. "I don't know what to do."

"If she finds out and you don't tell her and she moves away, we'll lose her forever. She won't trust us anymore."

"Us?"

"We come in a package, Birdie. We'll be her American friends who lied to her."

"Yeah, but you didn't lie."

"I know. But I'll be lying now." She pauses. "You want me to tell her?"

"No! I'll do it. Just let me find the right time, okay?" I look at Ally pleadingly. "Okay?"

She hands me Romeo's Valentine's card and gets off the

bed. "But soon. Really soon. You don't have much time left. This time next week you'll be in Chicago!"

"I know," I say, my eyes dropping.

It's silent for too long and I can feel Ally's eyes on me. "Okay," she says. "Come on. Let's go watch *Frozen*."

As Ally leaves the room, I pick up *When You Reach Me*, which is lying guiltily on the bed. "Traitor," I say and put the book back on my shelf. The mood ring on my finger has turned green but it might as well be black. I've been so focused on the mystery of Girl Detective this summer that I've completely avoided the case of Rose and Romeo.

Because once I tell her the truth, who knows what will happen next.

32

"**HELP ME,** Birdie," Zora whines. "Let's go get my bike."

"No," I say with my sternest big sister voice. "You are not bike racing!"

"Come on. Please!"

We're standing on our street, up the hill by Connor's house. It seems like all the neighborhood kids have gathered here this morning to race their bikes. Gainsborough Drive is pretty steep at this part but flattens out at the bottom in front of my house. Most of the racing kids are wearing helmets, and the boys are taking turns looking out for cars, but still, it's pretty dumb. And even if she were an excellent rider, Zora is way too young.

"Go play." I point to some of the younger kids playing in Connor's front yard. Zora crosses her arms against her chest stubbornly. "Come on. Just be a kid for once." I know I sound exasperated, but I *so* don't want to be on Zora duty right now.

Across the street, Rose is talking with Romeo. She's flirting with him. I can tell by the way she smiles and flips her hair.

I haven't told her yet. It's been four days since Ally found out about Romeo and me, and I still haven't told Rose. After putting it off for three days, I promised Ally I would do it last night.

So after dinner, I walked to Rose's house. I took the long way—up Chancery Lane, around Queen's Way, and back down Gainsborough Drive. The whole time, I looked at houses, especially the older ones, comparing them to Girl Detective's photo. I've studied this photo so many times over the past few days it's becoming emblazoned in my brain. The house was made of brick—I imagine red brick, but I can't be sure because it's in black-and-white. There were eight windows. Three little trees. One chimney. Walking along, I examined house after house. Some came close to matching but when I'd hold up the photo to compare, the trees would be in different places. Or the chimney was sitting on the wrong side of the roof. Or the windows . . . too many or too few. It was good to search, even though I couldn't find it. The searching kept my mind from other things. Like telling Rose.

Finally, I found myself standing on Rose's front porch where I rang the doorbell and waited. It was the first time in my life I rang Rose's bell and wished she wasn't home. No luck. She opened the door almost immediately and pulled me inside. "This is hilarious. Come see."

I joined Rose, her mom, and Simon at the kitchen table where Simon was showing them a video of his friend Teddy making a fool of himself over a girl. He was singing her this song and playing the ukulele. He can't really play, and he's a horrible singer. I mean he can't hit a note. The camera zoomed in on the girl, who was staring at him like he had a communicable disease or something. Of course, somebody posted it on YouTube. It was silly and embarrassing but really funny. Even Mrs. Ashcroft was laughing.

When it ended, Rose's mom wiped her eye with a tissue. "That poor boy," she said, then looked at me. "Can I get you some pudding, love?"

"Yes, please." Pudding means dessert in England, and Rose's mom makes excellent pudding.

As I sat down at the table, she went to the counter. "I feel so bad for Teddy. I really do."

"You laughed, Mum!" Simon said.

"Oh, I shouldn't have."

"Yes, you should have," Rose said. "It was so funny!" And then she actually grinned at her mother.

And her mom grinned back.

After all the yelling and stink bombing and violin burning, they were actually looking at each other like they hadn't for a very long time. Maybe it was because the violin was gone. Or maybe they called a secret truce. Whatever it was, I didn't care. It was a beautiful thing and I wished I had my Polaroid camera so I could capture the moment forever. As Mrs. Ashcroft placed her beautiful toffee cake and custard creation before me, I watched, mesmerized, as they were being happy.

I just couldn't tell Rose at a moment like that.

"No way!" Connor's yelling brings me back to our street, back to the bike racing. I turn and see him pointing at Moses, this daredevil kid who lives up on Queen's Way.

"What kind of derpy thing is that?!"

Moses is pushing this weird bike up the street. It has a

small front wheel and a big back one, a banana seat, and uneven handlebars. He flips his shades to the top of his head. "You just don't know bikes, Gomez."

"Right. I don't know bikes," Connor says. "Whatever."

Moses sits on the Frankenstein bike and pushes off. Everyone watches as he picks up speed and flies down the hill. The front wheel starts wobbling but Moses holds it together. He comes to a skidding stop in front of my house, turns around, and pumps his arms.

"What a maniac."

I turn to see Ally beside me, straddling her bike. "Yeah," I say. For a quiet, awkward moment, we watch Moses push his bike back up the hill.

"You didn't tell her, did you?"

My shoulders drop. "I couldn't," I confess.

"Birdie!"

"Shhh. Come over here." I walk over to Connor's side yard, away from everybody else. Ally follows and rests her bike against a tree. Her hands find her hips and she stares at me like I've committed a crime.

"Don't look at me that way," I say guiltily.

"How else am I supposed to look at you?" She turns to Rose. "Look at her! Flirting with Romeo. This is so uncool."

"I just . . . last night Rose and her mom were really getting along. They were happy. I was going to tell her. Really. I was. But I just couldn't ruin it."

She counts off on her fingers. "Saturday, Sunday, Monday, Tuesday. This is Wednesday. You're going to Chicago on Friday. What the heck, Bird?"

She never calls me Bird. Only Rose does that.

"You're always the one to tell me and Rose how to be," she says. "To be better and kinder and all that. Most of the time it's annoying but deep down, sometimes I'm glad you're like that. Because who else would tell me? I might be a holy horror if it weren't for you."

"Really?" I say, genuinely surprised.

"Yeah, but don't look happy! Because you're ruining it now. You won't even listen to me and you really have to. You have to!"

Rose is approaching. I see her coming from behind Ally. When Ally turns and sees her, she says it one more time. "You have to."

"Have to what?" Rose asks.

Ally stares at me mutely.

"Have to what, Bird?" Rose asks again. "What is it?"

"I have something to tell you," I say and my mouth goes dry.

"What?" She eyeballs the both of us. "What's with the serious?"

"It is serious," I say. "I didn't tell you something."

"Well, unless you murdered somebody, we're probably okay."

"No, we're not," I say. "We're not okay. I need to tell—"

"Birdie!" It's Zora, marching toward me, a crooked frown across her face. "Come on. I'm bored. If we're not riding bikes, let's go home!" She grabs my hand and pulls. I shake her off. Harder than I have to.

"Cut it out, Zora!" I say, too harshly. "Give me a minute, okay?"

I can tell that Zora's hurt but she's mad, too. "No! I want to go home now!"

"Please! Just go play! Five minutes!"

She stares at me, in the same way that Ally's been staring at me, like I'm a terrible person, and I just can't take it. "Go!" I yell and point to other side of Connor's yard.

Her lips narrow to a single line and she walks away. "What is up, Bird?" Rose says. "That wasn't cool."

"Nothing's cool!" I blurt out. "I'm a sucky friend and I'm really sorry." I seek out Rose's eyes and say, "Romeo doesn't like you, Rose. He likes me. He's liked me since Valentine's Day."

A hush descends upon our circle and I'm finding it hard to breathe. I watch Rose's face go pale as the news seeps into her skin and poisons her heart. "Why didn't you tell me?" she finally utters.

"I should have. I'm so sorry."

"Oh my gosh, I feel like such an idiot." Her eyes shift to Romeo and her face goes red. "How could you let me be such a . . . oh my gosh. Bird."

"I didn't want to hurt you."

"You lied to me."

"I didn't mean to." Our eyes lock. I can't look away. I'm afraid if I break our gaze, she'll never look at me again.

"Birdie!" It's Romeo's voice but I don't turn to him. I don't dare.

Ally grabs my arm. "Birdie!"

"What?!" My eyes reluctantly shift to Ally.

"Zora!" She's pointing toward the hill and for one long ridiculous moment, we are frozen in place, watching, as Zora starts rolling down the hill on Moses's Frankenstein bike.

"Zora!" I scream. "Zora, stop!"

But she doesn't. She actually pumps the pedals, making the bike go faster.

Everyone on the hill goes silent except for Moses, who calls out, "Hey, kid! Get off my bike!"

I want to blame him. Why did Moses leave his bike on the side of the road where Zora could get it? Why didn't one of the boys stop her?

I'm running now. Zora has stopped pedaling but the bike is accelerating anyway. Gaining speed. She's going too fast. The front wheel starts wobbling.

"Zora!" I yell and run as fast as I've ever run down the hill behind her. "Hold on!" And I realize she doesn't even have a helmet on.

As if in slow motion, Zora looks back at me. Her frightened face. I am a terrible sister. I would do anything to change this. But it's too late for that.

As Ally zooms past me, I watch the front wheel of the bike turn sideways and collapse. The Frankenstein bike bucks Zora off like it's a real live bronco. She's really flying now. I hear her scream before she lands headfirst on the asphalt.

"Zora!"

Ally gets there first. But I'm right behind her. "Go get Dad!" I yell. "Hurry!"

As Ally runs off, I kneel next to my sister, the bike in pieces behind us. There's blood on her head.

Gently, I put her head in my lap. "Zora, can you hear me?" She doesn't say anything. Her eyes are closed. A car approaches and stops in front of us. "Are you kids all right?" a grown-up voice calls out.

"Zora, speak to me. Please," I beg. "Please be okay."

33

THE FLUORESCENT lights buzz overhead, and in my mind, I'm tracing the geometric design on the floor tiles for the hundredth time. I've washed Zora's blood off my hands three times but I can still feel it. I can still see it on my shorts.

I'm a horrible sister. All I can think of is Zora's sad, mad little face looking up at me when I pointed my finger and sent her away. I was awful to my own little sister. Zora didn't mean any harm. She just wanted my attention. Like she always does. And I yelled at her in front of everyone in Connor's front yard.

I'm a horrible friend. If I had just told Rose about Romeo—and I could have told her about a million times— none of this would have happened. I wouldn't have been so mean to Zora. Ally wouldn't be mad at me for not telling Rose. And Rose might be speaking to me, which I seriously doubt she will ever do again.

I'm in a hospital waiting room on the fifth floor. Through the window, I can see that it's almost dark outside. A little girl wanders around the waiting room offering people imaginary cups of tea. Her father, in a tired voice, keeps telling her not to bother anybody, to come sit with him. It works temporarily. She sits patiently for a few minutes, starts fidgeting, then resumes her tea service. Over and over again.

I've had make-believe tea four times already, and still my throat burns. I'm buried in guilt and all I can do is sit here.

They've been moving Zora to a regular hospital room after all the hours we spent in emergency. I'm too worried to be bored.

"She's getting settled." I look up and see my mom. "Dad's with her."

"Is she going to be okay?" I ask.

"I think so," she says. "Come on. Let's get some food or something."

We walk to the elevator and Mom pushes the second floor button. Silently, we ride down three floors. I'm waiting for her to say something but she doesn't. When the elevator stops, we get out onto a quiet floor and I follow her down the hall. Guilty, guilty, guilty.

The hospital cafeteria is almost empty and we find a table by the window. Mom gets a cup of coffee and she buys me a turkey sandwich. I take a bite but don't feel like eating.

"Zora has a hairline skull fracture," Mom tells me. "And a concussion. So, it's not good."

"But she's going to be okay, right?"

"She should be," Mom says, and I notice the dark circles under her eyes. "She has to stay quiet and they want to watch her. She's going to have to stay here for a few days. That's mostly because of the concussion. They can't do much about the fracture. We'll just have to keep an eye on it and give it time to heal."

"Poor Zora," I say.

"Yeah." She takes a sip of coffee and rests her eyes on me. "What happened, Birdie?"

"I don't know. She got on that dumb bike. I didn't know she was doing it."

"Why would she do something like that? That doesn't sound like her."

"I don't know," I mumble. "She might have been upset."

Her eyes fall on me like a spotlight. "What would Zora have been upset about?"

When I was little, I found a bird's nest in our backyard. It had fallen out of a tree but the eggs inside weren't broken, so I picked them up and brought them into the house. Proudly, I opened my hands and showed the pale blue eggs to my mom. But instead of smiling, she frowned.

I could tell I had done something wrong but I didn't know what. When she explained that since I touched the eggs, the mama bird wouldn't want them anymore and they couldn't hatch without her, I didn't want to believe her. So I put the eggs in a box with a blanket, kept them warm, and wished and wished for the little birds to come out. When they never did, I began to wish for something else. I wanted to turn back time. If I could only go back to that day and not pick up those eggs, maybe those baby birds could have lived.

Looking at my mom across the hospital cafeteria table, I

want to turn back time again. To February 14. Instead of hiding Romeo's Valentine's card, I could have chosen to show it to Rose. It might have stung at first, but Rose would have moved on to like another boy and she wouldn't be mad at me. And today would have never happened. Instead of taking out my frustration on Zora, I could have been nice to her. We could have gone home, popped some popcorn, played a game. Anything not to have ended up here.

"What was Zora upset about?" Mom asks me again. "Weren't you watching her?"

"Yeah," I say. "Well, kind of . . . I mean . . . I tried but . . ."

"Hmm."

I hate it when she does that. Her *hmm* makes me feel more guilty. I try not to squirm in my seat.

"You've always been so good with Zora. I know we ask you to take on certain responsibilities with her, but we think that's good for you. And Zora thinks you hung the moon. She'd rather be with you than anyone else in the world."

"I know but—"

"Things are changing. I get that. But you only had to watch her for an hour. Is that too much to ask?"

I stare at my sandwich, unable to speak.

She leans forward, resting her elbows on the table. "Maybe it's being twelve, but sometimes it feels like you'd rather be with your friends than your family. And it hurts Zora's feelings. That's one reason I wanted us to go see your grandma. For some family bonding time." She pauses. "But you got what you wanted. We're not going to Chicago now."

"No, Mom! It's not what I wanted! Not like this!" My eyes

are stinging. "I'm sorry. I didn't want anything to happen to Zora. I'm so sorry, Mom." I wipe away a tear with the back of my hand.

We sit across from each other, this horrible tension between us, and Mom asks, "What's going on with you, Birdie?"

I let out a sigh that comes out more like a croak. "You'll think it's dumb."

She takes a long breath. "I won't. Tell me."

I start slowly. "It's just so much has been going on and Rose is mad at me and I was trying to do the right thing and I ended up doing the wrong thing . . . with Zora."

"What's Rose mad at you about?"

"Romeo," I say. "Rose likes Romeo."

"She's too young to like boys."

"That's not what Rose thinks."

"But what does this have to do with you?"

"Romeo likes me," I say and watch closely for her reaction.

Her mouth drops open. "He does?"

I nod. "Yeah. He likes me."

"How do you know?"

"He told me." I pause. "And gave me a Valentine's card."

"He did?"

"Yeah."

She sits back, taking this in, then blurts out, "You don't like him back, do you?"

I shake my head. "No. I mean, not like that."

"Oh gosh," Mom says. "A boy likes you. We're already there."

"But I told him we're just friends. Problem was, I never told Rose."

"You didn't want to hurt her."

"Exactly!" I exclaim. "But Rose . . . well . . . she's been flirting with Romeo all summer, thinking he liked her. But he didn't like her. And I knew. See?"

"Hmm. Does she know now?"

"I told her. Right before Zora's accident."

"Oh," Mom says, absorbing the tween angst that is currently me. "And how'd she take it?"

"Bad. And then Zora crashed." Mom winces when I say that. "Sorry, I mean, then I don't know. I didn't see her. But I'm pretty sure she hates me."

"What about Ally?"

"She's not so happy with me, either. She's the one who made me tell Rose."

"Sounds about right."

"Mom, Rose burned her violin."

Her eyes widen. "She didn't!"

"Set it on fire and floated it down the creek." I decide not to tell her about the lighter fluid, though.

"Does her mother know?"

"No," I say. "And you can't tell her. I just needed to tell you." And suddenly I feel the weight of all the things I've been carrying by myself this summer. The weight of Romeo, the violin, the mystery. I'm used to letting my mom share my load. Whenever I'd tell her a problem, it would somehow magically lighten. My eyes meet hers and I feel the tears coming.

"What is it, honey?" she asks.

"I'm scared, Mom," I say quietly. "I've always had Rose and Ally. I don't know who I am without them."

"Oh. Yes, you do." She reaches for my hand. "You absolutely do."

Shaking my head, I cry silently. "I don't think you're right," I whisper, and she strokes my hand like she always does when I'm sad.

I sit there feeling guilty and sad, and my mom doesn't say anything. She just looks at me like her eyes are the glue that holds me together. Finally, she says, "You know, there's a blessing and curse to having great friends like yours."

"What do you mean?" I ask, wiping my nose with a napkin.

"Best friends are wonderful. They make you feel like you always belong. But they can be a sort of crutch, too. You already have your friends, so you don't have to make friends with new people—people who might be interesting in different ways. You don't have to be brave on your own, because being with friends makes us braver. Maybe it's time for you to step out on your own for a while. And find out what the world's like for just you." She gives me a little smile. "And maybe there will be other kids going through the same thing as you are. Kids whose friends are going to different schools, too. You never know, it might turn out better than you think."

She might be right but I can't see that right now. Maybe, one day. I nod, wipe my nose again, and ask, "Can we see Zora now?"

34

"HELLO, MRS. ASHCROFT. It's Birdie. Is Rose there?" It's late to be calling but I've tried Rose's cell phone three times and she hasn't answered.

"Hi, Birdie," Rose's mom says. "How is your sister?"

"She's going to be okay," I say. "My dad is staying at the hospital with her tonight. She's mostly sleeping now."

Before my mom and I came home we visited Zora, and she was asleep most of the time except for once when she opened her eyes and said, "Hi, Birdie." Then she conked back out again.

"I'm very glad about that," Rose's mom says. "Please let your mother know if she needs anything at all to phone me."

"I will."

"Hold on a sec." I hear muffled voices in the background, and one of them sounds like Rose. "Sorry, Birdie," Mrs. Ashcroft says, speaking into phone again.

"Can I speak to Rose, please?" I ask her.

There's a pause when I can tell Rose's mom is thinking

what to tell me. "Rose wasn't feeling so well tonight and went to bed already. Can you talk with her tomorrow?"

"Sure," I say. "Will you tell her I called?"

"Yes, of course, I will."

"Thanks, Mrs. Ashcroft," I say and hang up the phone. I'm not used to adults lying to me. It usually works the other way around.

The next morning Mom and I go to the hospital early. I can hear Zora's voice from outside the room before we get there.

"Zora!" Mom says as we enter. "Look how good you look!" As Mom goes to hug her, Dad puts his arm around me and kisses the top of my head.

"You okay?" he says. I nod and lean into him.

Zora's eyes peek around Mom's neck, then go wide. "Peg Leg!" she exclaims. "You brought Peg Leg!"

I walk over to Zora, Peg Leg Fred in my hands. "I thought you might need a friend while you're here." I hand Peg Leg to Zora and she clutches him to her chest like he's the most treasured stuffed polar bear amputee in the world. "How are you feeling?"

"My head hurts and they poked me a lot, and look," she says, frowning at the needle taped to the inside of her arm. The needle is connected to a tube that connects to a transparent bag holding some sort of transparent fluid. The bag hangs on a metal stand that looks like a medical hat rack.

"I'm sorry," I say. "Does it hurt?"

"Not too much. But it hurt when she put it in."

"Astronauts have to be poked with needles sometimes. When they do tests on them after being in space," I say.

Zora considers this as thoughtfully as she can with a concussion. "I guess it will be okay when I'm an astronaut. Daddy says the crack in my head will make me even better at mathematics."

"He did?" I ask. "How's that?" I look at Dad standing at the foot of Zora's bed, looking tired but okay.

"Because," Zora says seriously, "there are mathematics molecules that float through the air and bump up against our skulls every day but can't get inside. Because there are no cracks. But since I have a crack, they get to go inside. And it's happening right now. Can you see them?"

"I think I can," I say convincingly. "I think I see some mathematical molecules seeping into your brain right now. Zora, you're going to be even smarter!"

"But only this one time," my mom warns. "And I hope your father told you, it won't work at all after the age of seven." She gives my dad an *Are you kidding me?* look. "So no more cracks, okay?"

Zora nods her little head agreeably. "No more cracks."

My parents go to the cafeteria for breakfast after I promise to stay with Zora responsibly. They can totally believe me this time.

I sit in the chair beside the bed and watch her have a full-blown conversation with Peg Leg about the accident and how she ended up in the hospital. "But don't worry, Peg Leg," she says and yawns. "I heard the doctor say I'm going home tomorrow." Her eyelids start drooping.

"Hey, Ace," I say. Zora smiles groggily. I used to call her Ace when she was a little kid. She had this airplane she would carry around all the time with a tiny toy pilot in the cockpit called Ace. But one day, she couldn't find him. We looked and looked but he was gone. Zora cried buckets over Ace until I told her what really happened—that Ace came to talk to me the night before he disappeared. He'd been recruited to go on a secret mission and didn't know when he'd return. He would try and come back one day but in the meantime, he asked if Zora would take care of his plane. And he would be very honored if, when she flies it, she would go by the name of Ace, too.

Dad is pretty much the only one who calls her Ace anymore. I haven't called her Ace in a long time.

"Did you see me crash?" she asks.

"Everybody saw you crash."

"I forgot to wear a helmet."

"I know. You should always wear a helmet."

"Yeah. Mom was mad at me about that."

"She wasn't mad," I say. "She was just worried."

"Okay. Can you see the mathematics molecules now?"

"Millions of them. They're all trying to get in your head. And they're very excited about it. By the time you leave the hospital, you're going to be a mathematical genius."

"But I'm already a mathematical genius," Zora says and manages a lazy smile before closing her eyes.

I look at her little fingers lying on top of the hospital sheet. Our nails are shaped exactly the same. "I'm sorry, Zora."

She doesn't open her eyes but says, "You are?"

"Uh-huh. I should have listened to you. I shouldn't have been so mean. I was really selfish and horrible. If I'd been a better big sister, none of this would have happened. So, I'm sorry."

She doesn't say anything, only pulls Peg Leg closer. I think she's fallen asleep when she says, "Birdie?"

"Yeah?"

"When I get out of the hospital . . ."

"Uh-huh."

"Do you want to go flying with me?"

"I do, Ace," I say. "I really do."

As Zora falls asleep, I stare out the window at the gray clouds rolling in. An American flag ripples outside. I feel so grateful that Zora is going to be okay. I'll make it up to her. I promise myself.

Leaning back in the chair, my eyes grow heavy. I suddenly feel so tired I can't keep them open. Slowly, I begin drifting. Floating, in fact. Back to the bottom of the creek. The water is clear and calm there. Just like before. Girl Detective's waving hair dances weightlessly above her head. I want to call out to her but I can't speak underwater. So I swim down. I push her hair away so I can see her blue eyes. So I can finally pull her to safety. As the curls part, I see her face. And gasp. Because it's not Girl Detective I'm looking at. It's Rose.

I have no idea how much time has passed when my mom comes back in the room and says, "Rose's mom just called me. They can't find her. She wasn't in her bed this morning. Do you know where she might be?"

35

THE CLOUDS have turned darker and it's sprinkling now. As I run past the pool, a sharp clap of thunder is immediately followed by three short bursts from Mrs. Franklin's whistle. I don't have to look to know she's clearing everyone out of the pool.

As soon as Dad and I got home (Mom stayed with Zora at the hospital), I went to Rose's house. Rose had not returned and her mom was really worried. She asked me if I knew anything—if Rose was upset. Or angry. I told her I did. I told her everything. "Maybe she's with Ally," she said. "That's probably it, but I can't reach anybody on the home phone or Ally's mobile."

"Why don't you try again," I said, "and I'll go look at the pool."

"Already looked. She wasn't there."

"I'll look again." Before she could object, I flew out the front door because I knew the only place Rose would be.

In minutes, I'm on the trail behind the clubhouse

heading for the woods. Halfway there, I see her. Rose. Walking toward me.

I stop, and when she sees me, she stops, too. We stare at each other before she turns and runs back into the trees.

"Rose!" I yell, and chase after her.

As I enter the woods, goose bumps bubble up on my arms. I'm not sure if they're from the chill or impending dread. The trail ends at the creek and as usual, I turn downstream and keep running. It doesn't take long before I'm at the tree bridge, stepping onto the fallen trunk.

"Stop!" Rose stands on the other side of the tree bridge, her hand held up. "You can't come on our island anymore."

"Come on. Let's talk about this," I say and take another step, the creek speeding past beneath me.

"I mean it. Traitors aren't allowed!"

"I'm not a traitor."

"You're the biggest kind of traitor!" There's a crack of thunder and Rose recoils, searching the sky.

"It's raining. Come on. Let's go. Your mom is freaking out."

"I don't care if she's freaking out. I'm not going anywhere with you."

"So you're just going to stand out here in the rain?" I know she would rather do anything than that.

"If I have to," she says uneasily.

"Okay, then. Let's stand here. I'm not moving until you talk to me."

She crosses her arms and glares at me—two stubborn chess pieces in a standoff.

"I don't like him, you know," I say. "I don't even like boys. This is completely dumb."

"Then why didn't you tell me? You've found all this time to look for some crazy dead girl this summer and you didn't find two minutes to tell me about you and Romeo?"

"I wanted to tell you a thousand times!"

"But you didn't." She stares at me from across the creek. "You let me look like an idiot with Romeo. It was so uncool. I would never do that to you."

"I know," I say, and it's true. She wouldn't.

"And then you take us on this wild goose chase looking for some girl who buried a box, which by the way, I wish we never found. She's dead. She's alive. I don't know and I don't care! What I do know is this was our last summer together. We'll never get it back. And you ruined it! You ruined it, Birdie!"

I don't know what to say. She's right. I did ruin the summer. I made the mystery of Girl Detective more important than anything else. And I don't know why. Something about the box, the clues, even the creepy knife seemed to hold the loosening bits of me in place. As if without them, I might have come apart like a poorly built bicycle. Even now, I can feel the photo of Girl Detective's house getting soaked in my back pocket. All I can say is, "I'm sorry."

Rose shrugs. "Yeah, well, me too. I'm sorry I trusted you. I'm sorry I've been your friend. I'm sorry I've wasted all my American time on you. Maybe it is time I go back to England. Maybe this America thing wasn't going to work out for me after all."

"You don't mean that. Even if you don't like me anymore, you like it here. You like Ally."

"Yeah, I do like her," Rose says. "I like her a lot." She glares at me poisonously. That hurts. I want to say something, anything, to make this better, but I see it in her eyes. My worst fear is coming true and I'm powerless to change it.

Keeping this secret from Rose was not a Greater-Good lie. It was a cowardly one. If I had told her right way, it would have been awkward and uncomfortable, sure. But only for a day. After that, we would have gone back to what was important. The friendship between Ally, Rose, and me.

I feel like an idiot because I've been one.

Heavy raindrops begin to fall. I know this has never been about Romeo. This has been about me. I was so afraid of hurting Rose that I really hurt her. By withholding the truth for so long, the truth became toxic. Each day, it became more and more volatile, like an unstable isotope. Building up inside me like a bomb.

"Please, Rose." I say it loudly because the rain is pouring down now. "I don't want you to leave this way."

Rose stands like a stone. I see the hurt in her eyes and don't know if it's rain or tears running down her face.

"It's bad enough you're leaving, but we can handle that." I'm practically shouting now. "We can talk or e-mail or Skype every day. But you can't *leave me* leave me. You can't do that! I screwed up. Totally! But I never meant to hurt you." Raindrops are streaking my face but tears are, too. "You are my best friend, Rose. You and Ally. Ever since that day in first grade.

Ever since you came to us. And I don't know what I'm going to do without you."

Rose is drenched. And so am I.

"And boys suck," I yell. "We can't let this happen to us over a dumb boy!"

Her eyes slightly soften.

"I've learned my lesson," I say. "No more secrets."

She stares at me, not giving in.

So I add, "And no more clues."

"Promise?" she says.

"Promise." We stand there just looking at each other. For a moment, there is no space or time. No rain. No England. No Romeo. Until Rose looks up to the sky. "It's raining really hard, Bird."

"Yeah, I know," I say. "Let's get out of here!"

As Rose takes a step onto the tree bridge, the loudest crack of thunder I have ever heard descends like a monster from the sky.

"Bird!" Rose yells, her eyes reaching their enormous limits. I swing around. The tree behind me is on fire. Cracking. Hissing. Falling.

My eyes return to Rose, her arms reaching out to me. "Come on!" she yells. And I do. I sprint across the tree bridge, grab on to her arms, and we scurry up onto the island together as the smoking tree behind us falls. Creaking and moaning, it drops to the forest floor, crushing the spot where I was standing. Demolishing the tree bridge. Dying on our island's shore.

"Holy crap," Rose utters as we stand together, holding

each other's arms tightly. The part of the tree that fell onto the island is on fire, but the rain quickly devours it.

"You all right?" I ask.

"Yeah," she says quietly. "You?"

"Yeah." I can't take my eyes off the smoking tree. "Holy crap is right."

We stand there hypnotized by the hissing and groaning tree as the hard rain turns soft. "Did you hear that?" I ask.

"What?"

"Listen."

She does and then yells, "Ally!"

"Rose!" Ally calls back.

"Al!" I shout, too.

Ally appears on the other side of the creek, running down the path toward us. Her face fills with disbelief as she approaches the smoking behemoth lying before her. "What the—" Her eyes flip to us. "You guys okay?"

I look at Rose and she looks back at me. "Are we okay?" I ask her.

She makes me suffer, for just a second, then says, "Yeah. We're okay. We're okay now."

Ally disappears, then reappears on the top of the fallen tree, like she's the queen of the jungle. "Cool," she says, calling down to us. "New tree bridge."

Rose grins. "Ally would see it like that."

36

I KNOW I promised Rose. And I didn't lie to her. Really.

When I came home from the island, soaked from the rain, I pulled the wet photo of Girl Detective's house from my back pocket and read the clue on the back one last time:

> *Good work, detective.*
> *You're almost home.*
> *The evidence you need*
> *Lives where I used to*
> *Upstairs. Second on right,*
> *Creaky floorboard by the bookshelf.*
> *Thank you.*

In that moment I realized I would never peek under that squeaky floorboard and discover the last clue that might solve everything. And that was going to have to be okay. Because the box, the clues, even Girl Detective, they were all ancient history. Rose, Ally, and I, we were right now. And I wasn't going to waste another minute of it.

I took the clue box out from under my bed and opened it. Inside, I saw the Allman Brothers Band ticket, the weird knife, and the yellowed paper clues. Slipping the mood ring from my finger, I returned it to them. Then I placed the black-and-white photo right on top.

As I gazed at it all, one last time, I said a silent good-bye to Girl Detective. I wished her well, wherever she was, and closed the lid. My eyes fell upon the words that started it all, *Open If You Dare* written in bold marker on the silver surface, and I couldn't help but grin. Because I dared. I opened the box. I followed the clues. But it was done now. I placed the box back under my bed and planned to bury it on the island again once Rose was gone. It would almost be like it never happened.

And it worked. Over the next week, I hardly thought about it. Really.

Zora was doing better, recovering, and Rose, well, she was leaving in two days. We had had the very best week together. All of us. Even me and Zora. And Girl Detective was becoming a phantom.

Until today.

I was walking back from Rose's, after helping her with some last-minute packing, and found myself stopping at the halfway point between our houses. I don't know why my eyes were drawn to the green ivy or the brick chimney or the old shingled roof. Or the tall trees leaning dangerously over that roof. Or the bushes, the flowers, and all those plants. But they were.

And the pieces suddenly came together.

Back at my house, I call both of my friends. I ask them to meet me halfway between my house and Rose's. But before I leave, I open the box and retrieve two items. I slip the mood ring in my front pocket and the black-and-white photo into my back one.

Less than half an hour later, we're standing on the street in front of Mrs. Hale's house.

"Okay, I know I promised but don't be mad." I'm looking at Rose, not Ally as I pull the black-and-white photo out of my back pocket.

"I thought we weren't doing this anymore," Ally says.

"You did promise," says Rose.

"I know. I know I did. But hear me out. Please."

It takes a second but Rose says, "Okay."

"I wasn't looking. I swear. I put the box away. I was even going to bury it again after . . . you know. But . . ." I hold out the photo and place it in Rose's reluctant hand. "But look." I point to Mrs. Hale's house. To the eight windows and the three trees and the chimney in exactly the right place. "Why didn't I see it before?"

"Cuz that yard's like a bird's nest and that ivy might as well be digesting the house," Ally says. And I feel a bit better because she's right. It's hard to believe the house in the photo could actually be this house in real life.

As we look back and forth from the photo to the house, nobody says anything until Rose sighs. "Yeah, I guess this is it."

I want to pump my fist I'm so happy, but I choose to suppress it. Instead I look at Rose and Ally sincerely and say,

"We don't have to go in. It can be enough just to know we found it." I'm lying of course. But in a way I'm not.

Ally's eyes turn toward the house while Rose's baby blues plant themselves on me. "I can't believe I'm going to say this. But come on. Let's go solve this thing."

I ring the doorbell while my friends stand behind me on Mrs. Hale's front porch.

When the door creaks open and Mrs. Hale appears, she asks, "Yes?"

"Hi, Mrs. Hale," I say. "We were wondering if we could come in for a minute?" We came up with a plan between the street and Mrs. Hale's front porch. Once we get inside, Rose and Ally will distract Mrs. Hale while I sneak upstairs to find the room with the squeaky floorboard. Yeah, I'm going to do that.

"What? Wait. Hold on a minute. Come in. Come in." Mrs. Hale disappears and slowly, I push the front door open and step inside.

It's not what I expected.

Unlike the outside of the house that's in a general state of overgrown disarray, the inside is orderly and quite beautiful. Stepping onto the polished hardwood floor, we gaze at the ornate entryway, the old paintings, the Chinese vases, and the curio cabinet containing delicate figurines.

Mrs. Hale reappears from around the staircase, her hands to her ears. "Now I can hear you," she says brightly. "I'm so bad about wearing these things." And I realize she just put her hearing aids in. She smiles at us. "Please come sit down. To what do I owe the pleasure of this visit?"

As she leads us into her living room, with the elegant rug and the wall-to-ceiling bookshelves, I realize something else, too. She doesn't answer me when I speak to her not because she's mean or a racist. She doesn't answer me because she's practically deaf.

We line up on her sofa like three little peas and Mrs. Hale sits across from us in a regal red chair. "Birdie, I know." Shocker, she knows my name. "And Rose." Then she looks at Ally. "What's your name, dear?"

"I'm Ally," Ally says happily. If she had a tail, it would be wagging.

"Where are my manners? Would you like something to drink?" she asks.

"No—" I start to say before Rose cuts in. "That would be lovely, Mrs. Hale."

"Wonderful. I was just going to make some tea," Mrs. Hale says and shows off what is actually a very nice old lady smile. "I hear you're moving back to London soon, Rose."

"In two days."

"Oh, so soon! I'm sure we'll all be sad to see you go. Especially your friends here. The three of you seem to be thick as thieves." The hint of a far-off look makes me think she's remembering her thick-as-thieves friends from long ago. "You'll be drinking lots of tea over there," she says. "In England. The English people drink an extremely large amount of tea, you know." She stands. "Be right back."

As she leaves the living room, we huddle together and start whispering.

"She's really nice," Ally says.

"Really nice," Rose says. "How come we didn't know that?"

"So that's great. She's nice." And truly, under other circumstances, I would have taken the time to marvel over this unexpected development. But I've got a mystery to solve. "When she comes back with the tea, I'm going to make my move. All you have to do is distract her."

"Would you girls like some cookies?" Mrs. Hale calls from the kitchen.

"Yes, please," Ally yells back, then leans in and whispers, "I'm not so sure this is a good idea after all."

"It was never a good idea, Al," says Rose. "Nothing about that has changed. But we're here."

Mrs. Hale walks back into the living room and places a tray carrying old-fashioned tea cups, a small pitcher of milk, a bowl of sugar cubes, and a plate of cookies on the coffee table in front of us.

"Tea won't take long," she says and leaves us again.

Ally grabs a sugar cube and pops it in her mouth. "Why don't we just ask her about clue box girl—"

"Girl Detective," I correct her. And for the first time since finding the house, I start to wonder how Mrs. Hale and Girl Detective might be connected.

"Whatever," Ally garbles. "Let's just ask her."

"What if she's dead," I whisper because we really don't know that part yet. "She still might be dead."

"Ruthie's not dead," Rose whispers back. "Girl Detective's not dead."

"Either way, we'll show our hand," I say.

"Our hand of what," Rose says and rolls her eyes.

"Tea!" Mrs. Hale sails back in holding a teapot. She fills our cups and we awkwardly lift cups and saucers from the tray. Ally rests hers on the coffee table and scoops out six sugar cubes with her fingers (and the tongs are right there!) and plops them into her cup.

"You have a beautiful home, Mrs. Hale," Rose says.

"Why, thank you, Rose. It's full of years and years of stuff. A lifetime's worth." Mrs. Hale pours her own cup of tea and sits back down in the chair. "One day you girls will have a lifetime of stuff. But always remember, stuff is nice but it's not what's really important."

"No, it's not," Ally says. And I know she's thinking about her dad.

I clear my throat. "May I use the restroom, Mrs. Hale?"

"Yes, of course, Birdie." She points toward the entryway. "It's just on the other side of the stairs."

I can see the stairs from here. So can Mrs. Hale if she looks in that direction.

Rose pinches the back of my arm and I shoot her a look. Carefully, I place my cup and saucer on the coffee table and get up from the sofa.

"I bet the neighborhood has changed a lot since you've been here," Rose says lightly, calling Mrs. Hale's full attention her way. As Mrs. Hale answers, I walk toward the bathroom, peek over my shoulder, then tiptoe onto the stairs. The third step creaks but I keep going, hoping that even with her hearing aids, Mrs. Hale is hearing challenged. I don't breathe until I've made it to the top.

Reaching into my pocket, I pull out the mood ring and slip it on my finger. Somehow it connects me to Girl Detective. If she's with me, even in spirit, maybe I won't get caught.

The stairway leads to an upstairs hallway. I look down at my sneakered feet, beg them to tread lightly and start walking. The door to the first room on the right is open. It looks like a guest room, beautifully decorated like the rest of the place. It occurs to me that this is a very grown-up house. Maybe a kid has never lived here. And suddenly, I'm filled with panic. What if I've got it all wrong? What if this isn't Girl Detective's house at all?

I can hear Rose's reassuring voice in the background, deep in conversation with Mrs. Hale, while I picture Ally eating cookie after cookie and nodding her head.

As I approach the second door on the right, the words of the last clue echo in my brain:

Upstairs. Second on right,

Creaky floorboard by the bookshelf.

The door is closed. It feels weird, kind of wrong, to open a closed door in a strange house. As my hand wraps around the knob, I hear Mrs. Hale's voice from below. "I think I have a photograph of that upstairs," she says, and I can hear her walking toward the stairs.

"No! That's okay," Rose calls out. "You don't need to go upstairs for that!" Her voice rises on the word *upstairs* in warning.

"No trouble at all," Mrs. Hale says, and I hear her footsteps begin climbing the wooden stairs.

I can almost see the top of her head when I turn the doorknob to the second door on the right and fling myself inside. Quietly, I close the door behind me and lean against it, my heart pounding like a jackhammer.

The clicking sound of Mrs. Hale's shoes approaches and my whole body clenches. What if she finds me?! I close my eyes and listen as she passes by the door. After a moment, the clicking stops and everything goes silent. I dare not move. Then the clicking returns and it stops right outside my door. "Now where is that?" I hear her ask herself quietly. My eyes are glued to the doorknob. For any sign of it turning. She's on the other side of the door, just standing there. I can almost hear her breathing.

"Oh, I know," she says again, and the clicks continue. Soon she calls out, "Found it!" and the clicking heels head back downstairs again.

I exhale and lean back on the door like I might die. Finally, I open my eyes.

And discover that a girl lived here after all.

There's a twin bed with a pink-and-blue flowered bedspread and stuffed animals piled up against a pillow. There's a small desk with lots of different colored pens in a large pencil holder. And shelves and shelves of books.

Tiptoeing around the bed, I momentarily lose myself in all those books. Most I recognize from later editions but some I do not. They're carefully organized, alphabetically. Just like I do it. I see *James and the Giant Peach*, then scan further down to find *A Wrinkle in Time*.

This was Girl Detective's bedroom. I know that now. I examine the floorboards between the bed and a bookshelf, and gently press down on one with my sneaker. No squeak on the first one. No squeak on the second one. Then, squeak. Kneeling down, I touch the third floorboard with my hand. It squeaks again but I can't pull it up.

Hurrying to the desk, I find a letter opener among the bunch of pens. It feels like a dagger in my hand as I carry it back to the squeaky floorboard. Slipping the letter opener between the planks, I try to pry it open, but the floorboard doesn't shift. I move to the other side, slip it in just right, push in and pull up at the same time and . . .

There. It lifts open. I remove the piece of flooring as quietly as I can and uncover a small compartment underneath containing only one thing.

A small yellowed envelope.

I set the board gently on the floor beside me and reach inside. The envelope feels like a sacred artifact in my hand. I should put it in my pocket and make for the door, because no one could be in a restroom for this long. But I don't. I feel like I'm supposed to open it here. Open it now. And after all, I have a letter opener in my hand.

I slip the dagger beneath the fold of the envelope and run it through, creating a slit, exposing the letter inside. My fingers reach in and pull out a folded white letter. The mood ring on my finger has gone purple, and the way I feel now, purple must mean happiness because I'm here. I've found what I've been looking for. I've reached the end of the line. I can feel it.

This is where Girl Detective has been leading me all along. I unfold the note and press it out flat on the floor. This is what it says:

Dear Detective Paulson,
Congratulations. You did it!
You are smarter than you look!
By now you must know that Martin Smith killed Ruthie
  Delgado.
I know this because I saw him stalking her on more than
  one occasion.
When she disappeared,
When she never showed up at the Allman Brothers concert,
I knew what happened.
Why didn't you?
I am dead now. Martin Smith killed me, too.
Because I went looking. I went asking.
Why doesn't anyone ever believe a twelve-year-old girl?
I hope you feel just a little guilty now.
And I hope you had to work extra hard to find this final
  clue.
Otherwise, I'm a better detective than you are.

*Would you please hightail it over to Smith and Sons and
arrest Martin Smith?*
I'll be watching.

Yours Truly,
A Certain Dead Girl

"Excuse me," a voice says, and I turn toward the door,
the clue and the daggerlike letter opener in my hand. A
woman is standing in the doorway with an odd expression on
her face. Her curly red hair is pulled back and her blue eyes
are searing a hole through me. And I realize I'm looking at a
certain dead girl.

I should be scared. I should want to run. But I don't. I just
stare at her as the words slowly form in my brain:

Hello, Girl Detective.

37

IT'S THE weirdest moment of my life. I'm looking at a grown woman who's been a girl—and probably a dead one—in my head all summer.

Also, she's caught me red-handed. There's no doubt about that. But she doesn't make a move to call the police. She just looks at me and I can tell words are slowly forming in her brain, too.

I hold up my hands, surrendering, like in an old western movie. My right hand clenching the clue, my left hand wrapped around the letter opener.

"You've got to be kidding me," she utters.

I shake my head slowly. "No, I'm pretty much not." We search each other's eyes. Then I ask, "You're her, right?"

"Yeah," she says slowly. "Yes, I am." The corners of her mouth curl up slightly.

"This was your room."

"Uh-huh." She sits down on the bed and reaches out to me. "Let me see it."

I hand her the letter and watch as she reads it through.

"I'd almost forgotten about this." Her eyes turn to me. "And my ring!" she says with real delight. I pull the mood ring off my finger and hold it out. She takes it (like it's a sacred artifact), slips it on her ring finger, and lets out a burst of laughter. "It doesn't fit anymore. Of course it doesn't."

"I knew it was a kid's ring. Right when we found it."

As she gazes at the ring, I realize this is not just Girl Detective from my dream, with the waving hair and the blazing blue eyes. This version of her, the current one, looks familiar. Not dream familiar, real-life familiar. But where have I seen her before? Who is this G.D.?

She notices me staring. "Why are you looking at me like that?"

"I don't know. Don't I know you? I mean, now. In real life?"

"Hmmm. I don't think so," she says. "Are you a reader? Do you go to the local library?"

"All the time." And then it hits me. "You're the mystery writer! The lady on the poster! You're having a signing—"

"Today. I had a book signing today. At the library. That's why I'm here." With everything going on, I completely forgot about the book signing at the library. Then she adds, "But I also came to visit my mom."

It takes a second for this to sink in. Mrs. Hale wasn't always old. She was probably my mom's age when Girl Detective was twelve. The timeline fits. Of course it does. I just couldn't see it until now. "Mrs. Hale's your mom?"

Girl Detective smiles. "And you got past her to find the final clue. Good job, Nancy Drew. What's your name?"

"Birdie. Birdie Adams."

"Nice to meet you, Birdie Adams. I'm Emily McAllister."

I so badly want to call her Girl Detective but instead I say, "Nice to meet you, Ms. McAllister."

"Oh, call me Emily. Everybody does. And besides, I think you've earned the right."

That feels kind of weird because she's a grown-up but I say, "Okay."

"You couldn't have found the first clue," she says, "because I mailed that to Detective Paulson at the police station. So . . . you found . . . the box?"

I nod.

"Which was the second clue."

"I thought it had to be the second clue," I say. "Because how could anybody find it otherwise."

"How *did* you find it?" she asks. "You must be some detective."

"I'm a terrible detective!"

Girl Detective, I mean Emily, grins at me. "As it turns out, so was I. Nobody killed Ruthie. Nobody killed anybody." She pauses. "Does it make me a bad person that I was a little disappointed when I realized that?"

Mrs. Hale is surprised to see us walking down the stairs together. "When did you get home, Emily?"

"Not long ago," Emily says. "I was showing Birdie something upstairs." What an excellent liar. I love this woman already!

If Rose and Ally could see themselves—their gaping mouths and surprised eyes—they would bust up laughing.

As we walk into the living room, I look at my friends and announce, "Meet Girl Detective!"

"Who's Girl Detective?" Emily asks as we sit down, joining them.

"It's a long story," I say, and Rose, Ally, and I start telling them of our adventure. Of finding the clue box on the island and finding the next clue in the Gillans' mailbox. Of going to Smith and Sons and seeking out Mr. Smith in the nursing home in Decatur.

"And then I found this," I say and pull the black-and-white photo from my back pocket. I feel embarrassed that it's crumpled but I hand it to Emily anyway.

She takes the picture and shows it to Mrs. Hale. "Look, Mom! Remember when the house looked like that?"

Mrs. Hale puts on her glasses and examines the photo closely. "Where did you get this?" she asks me.

I smile at Emily knowingly.

"That book was still there?" she says. "After all this time!"

"In the secret room. In a stack under the Anne of Green Gables train."

"I can't believe it."

"What is she talking about, Emily?" Mrs. Hale asks, confused.

Emily gives me an admiring look. "You really are some detective."

"She was obsessed," Ally says.

"Completely," adds Rose.

"Yeah," I say, "but we followed the clues to here. To the

final clue. I had to get to the end. Even though we already knew that Ruthie Delgado's alive—"

"Well, you don't know she's *still* alive," Emily says. "It's been forty years."

"But we do!" Rose says. "We called her."

"You did?"

The three of us nod together in our lineup on the sofa.

"She thought we were crazy," I say.

"She thought *you* were crazy," Ally corrects.

"Well, yeah," I say. "But it was her. No doubt. Lives in Michigan now."

"Really," Emily says. "Ruthie Delgado lives . . ."

I focus on her like a real detective would and ask, "So what really happened?"

She turns serious and says, "If anyone deserves to know the truth, it's you three." She looks at her mother. "Mom, may I have a cup of tea?"

"Here, have mine," Mrs. Hale says and slides over her teacup. "I want to hear every bit of this."

"Okay." Emily McAllister opens with a storyteller's grin. "It was a dark and stormy night."

"Really?" I ask. "Isn't that an old Victorian novel cliché?"

"Yes, but clichés are clichés for a reason," Emily answers. "The night Ruthie Delgado never showed up to the Allman Brothers concert was the night this really began. And it *was* a dark and stormy night. But let's go back.

"Ruthie was a teenager, several years older than me, and maybe the coolest girl in the neighborhood. I watched how she did things and tried to copy her. The way her hair effortlessly floated behind her. The way she walked with such confidence and flair. She was really something."

"She wasn't that great," Mrs. Hale mutters.

"Mom, let me tell the story."

Mrs. Hale shrugs. "Continue."

"Okay, so Ruthie never came home from the concert and I was sure I knew what happened. This guy, Martin Smith, kept following her around. I had watched him. A lot. And Ruthie tried to get him to leave her alone but he just kept on bugging her. And it wasn't normal bugging. There was something scary about Martin. And I could tell Ruthie was scared of him. Then one day, I saw Martin corner Ruthie at the pool and ask her to go to the concert. With him! Ruthie said she was already going to the concert and that she would never go anywhere with Martin. And that she never wanted him to talk to her again. She really told Martin what was what. Even though I could tell she was shaking."

"That boy was trouble," Mrs. Hale says. "No two ways about it."

Emily looks at her mom. "You knew he was trouble, too? I thought I was the only one."

"Darling, everyone knew," Mrs. Hale says, her eyebrow lifting.

"Well, that might have changed things," Emily says, almost to herself, before looking at us again. "Anyway, when Ruthie never came home from the concert—"

"Because she never went to the concert," I add.

"Exactly. Everybody was so concerned about her, I just knew that it was Martin. So. On a hunch, I snuck into the

Delgados' house and found the unused ticket in Ruthie's room—"

"You snuck into their house!" Mrs. Hale says.

"Mom, it was a hundred years ago. Relax. And I found the ticket, so I knew Ruthie never even made it to the concert in the first place. And that evening, before the concert, I had seen Martin hanging around her house. And Martin was a butcher. Or at least a butcher's son. So when we heard that Ruthie was missing the next day, I just put two and two together. There was no doubt in my mind. Martin Smith killed Ruthie Delgado."

"You thought he killed her?" exclaims Mrs. Hale.

Emily nods. "Of course I did. And I told Detective Paulson everything because it was his job to investigate murders. But he just ignored me and—"

"You went to the police station!"

"Yes, Mother. I went to the police station." Emily leans toward us and speaks more softly. "She acts like she was paying attention, but none of the parents did back then. We kids did whatever we wanted."

I try and suppress a grin as Mrs. Hale says loudly, "What did you say?"

Emily continues. "I was just saying that nobody believed me, so I decided to go after Martin Smith myself."

"You didn't!" Mrs. Hale says, shaking her head.

"I did! But I realized that by facing the killer alone I might be feeding myself to the lions, so I mailed Detective Paulson the letter and then hid all the other clues. Because I was mad. And he didn't believe me. And I was going to make Detective

Paulson work for it. Even if it meant I was walking into my sure and certain death."

"Your imagination," says Mrs. Hale.

"Well, that part worked out," she says and gestures to the books along the shelf behind her. I look at them and register that she wrote them. All of them. So yes, I guess her imagination really did work out for her. "Anyway, when I couldn't find Martin, I kind of made a scene at Smith and Sons. I confronted his father, the real butcher, and he got pretty angry at me. Didn't like the idea of me accusing his son of killing Ruthie Delgado, I guess."

"Yep, he sure remembers you," Rose says.

"Well, that is regrettable," Emily says. "But unavoidable. But then a month later, boy was I surprised when Ruthie showed up. Alive! The rumor was that she ran away with some boy and that her father tracked her down and brought her home. But I had worked so hard on the clues. I had funneled all of my paranoid speculation into them. All of my twelve-year-old brilliance." She grins. "I thought about digging them up. Collecting them again but I kept putting it off. For some reason, I wanted them to be out there. To have a life. Even though no one would ever find them." She looks at me. "I wasn't expecting you."

"I have a question," Mrs. Hale says to her daughter.

"What, Mom?"

"Why in the world didn't you come to me?"

Famous, grown-up author Emily McAllister suddenly looks twelve again. The way we all look when our moms ask us something we just can't answer. "I don't know," she mutters. "I just thought . . ."

"If you had come to me, I could have told you everything," Mrs. Hale says. "We all knew that Ruthie ran off with her boyfriend that night. It wasn't a very happy home, the Delgado house. I felt bad for her when her dad found her and dragged her back."

"Really?" Emily asks. "You knew all that?"

"Of course I did. I'm your mother."

While Girl Detective takes this new information in, I can't help but think about my own mom. For some reason, and I'm not sure why, I haven't told her about any of this. Nothing about the clues, the box, or the girl from the past who sent them to us. Is this what happens to twelve-year-old girls? We stop telling things to our mothers?

"What happened to Martin Smith?" Ally asks like she's really interested. "We never found out."

"Martin died," Mrs. Hale says flatly.

"He did?" Emily asks. "How?"

"Struck by lightning," she says. "Anyone want more tea?"

"Yes, please!" Emily says.

Rose's mouth drops open and her eyes grow bigger than I've ever seen them. "Lightning?"

"Lightning." Mrs. Hale nods. "It happens, you know."

"Mom. Tea. Please."

Mrs. Hale lets out a little sigh. "Fine, then." She rises wearily and heads toward the kitchen. "What I have to do, your poor old mother." But there's a smile in her voice. I can tell she's kidding.

Emily turns to us dryly. "What a drama queen."

38

"**I WAS** a morbid creature," Emily says as she studies the skinning knife that had been hiding in the Gillans' mailbox for the past forty-four years.

It's later that afternoon and I've returned by myself. Ally has gone with Rose to help her pack her carry-on for the plane. I've laid out all the clues and clue elements (the original clue box, the mood ring, the concert ticket, the knife, and the photograph) on a table in the screened-in porch off the back of Mrs. Hale's house. Emily McAllister and I sit beside each other on a bench.

"I'm amazed by all of this," she says. "I'm amazed I did it, but I'm really amazed that you were able to make sense of it. What an interesting twist to my trip."

"I have a question," I say.

"Okay. Shoot."

"Why do you think you did it?"

"The clues?" she asks.

"Yeah," I say. "It sounds like you were as obsessed making them up as I was obsessed finding them."

"Well . . ." She thinks about it for a second. "I guess because being twelve was hard for me. I was different. You know, kind of introverted. I felt like nobody understood me, like I would never fit in. And looking back, I think making up the clues gave me something to hold on to while I was growing into who I was going to be. Does that make sense?"

"Yeah. It makes a lot of sense. And you really grew up here?"

"Well, you saw the room."

"That was weird. I mean, it hasn't changed in a long time and you don't live here anymore."

"I know," she says. "My mom is strange that way. After I left for college, I thought she might redecorate it, but she didn't. It's like a museum piece from the 1970s."

"Where do you live now?"

"Brooklyn. In New York. My husband is a professor there and my office overlooks the East River."

"No kids?" I ask.

"No kids. A cat named Jeremiah. And my books."

"You've written lots of them?"

"Lots," she says. "With an imagination like yours, maybe you'll be a writer, too."

I roll that over in my brain. "I don't think so. That's not really me. I'll probably be a teacher." I hesitate, then add, "Or a librarian."

"Librarians are awesome!" she exclaims. "A librarian really inspired me when I was your age. I don't know if I would have been a writer had it not been for her. She worked at the local library. Where I signed today."

"Mrs. Thompson told me about her. Mrs. . . ."

"Mrs. Parsons," Emily says.

"Right! Mrs. Thompson said people thought she was mean but she wasn't."

"Well, she was mean to some people, but if you were a reader, if you loved books, Mrs. Parsons loved you. She opened a whole world to me with books. She made suggestions. She encouraged me. That's why I come back and sign at the library as often as I can. In honor of Mrs. Parsons."

She grins, then stands up. "I'll be right back." As I wait patiently for her return, I gaze at the clues and artifacts arranged on the table. I know that they bind us together. But I also realize something else. That there are people like me out there in the world. As much as I will always be connected to Rose and Ally, I will find those other people, too. I know this now because I've just met one.

Emily returns with a book in her hand. "This might be a little old for you, but I think you can handle it."

The book is her new book. The one she was signing at the library today. She opens it and grabs a pen off the table. "Thanks, Girl Detective," I say.

"Girl Detective! You never told me what that means!"

I can feel myself blushing. "It's you," I say. "You're Girl Detective."

"What?" she asks, confused.

"That's what we called you from the very start. Right after we opened the box. You became our Nancy Drew. Our Girl Detective."

She smiles. "Okay. Girl Detective. I can get behind that."

Then Girl Detective opens her book and writes something inside. When she finishes, she hands the book to me. "Thank you, Birdie," she says. "Thanks for solving my mystery. And thanks for making me feel like a twelve-year-old again."

39

THE NEXT day, Rose, Ally, and I climb over the new, charred tree bridge to the island. We carry certain items in our hands. This is our last full day together.

They came to my house for breakfast. Dad made us Mickey pancakes, and Zora sat in Rose's lap the whole time. It made me realize that Zora will miss Rose, too. Mom took a Polaroid picture of the four of us shoving pancakes in our faces, one of our best pictures ever.

On our way to the island, we passed Mrs. Hale's house. Girl Detective was going back to New York today. She gave me her e-mail and told me to keep in touch. Now that I will be corresponding to New York and London, it's time to get an e-mail address.

We also passed Romeo, Joey, and Connor riding their bikes. They stopped and Rose said her good-byes to them. She seemed really okay with everything. She even pulled Romeo aside and whispered something into his ear.

I am so glad all of that is over.

Ally carries the pool-house shovel over her shoulder, and

I carry the clue box and a small plastic bag. Rose holds a canvas bag with a drawstring handle. We step onto the island and walk to our usual spot under the willow tree.

"Where should we do it?" Ally asks.

"How about up there?" I say, pointing toward the bush at the high point on the island. "Where we found it."

"Yeah," Rose says. "It should be there."

We hike up to the spot where we dug up the clue box at the beginning of the summer. The hole is mostly filled in now. So Ally starts digging.

It's a hot, sunny day, so I sit down on the grass. Rose joins me and we listen to the sounds of the shovel.

"You ready?" I ask.

"Yeah," Rose says, then gives me a pout. "But no. Not really."

"Maybe we can come visit," Ally says between digs.

"Or you can come visit us," I say.

"Sure," Rose says and draws little circles with her finger in the grass. We sit there silently, weighed down by the knowledge of what's coming next. What's coming tomorrow. And then what's coming after that. Rose looks up, her blue eyes more vulnerable than I've ever seen, and says, "You won't forget me, will you?"

Ally throws down the shovel and sits beside us, forming our familiar circle. "Are you kidding?"

"It happens," Rose says. "People move away and things change. It just happens."

"It won't happen with us," I say.

"Not a chance," says Ally.

"You promise?" Rose asks.

"We promise," Ally and I say at the same time.

We look at one another as if we are searing this moment into our minds. So we can reach back to it time and time again like a talisman or a good luck charm.

"And in ten years, we'll be twenty-two," I say.

"Or twenty-one," says Ally.

"Either way, we'll be old enough to meet here again. No matter what." I open the silver *Open If You Dare* clue box and place it between us. "This will forever be our *Open If You Dare* box. Our time capsule. To remind us—"

"Of us," Rose says.

"Of us," echoes Ally.

"As a testament to our last summer together." I smile, then ask Ally, "What do you got?"

She digs into her shorts pocket and pulls out two things. She holds up the first item—a red, white, and blue tassel— and says, "This came off Joey's dad's convertible on the Fourth of July—the day you guys saved me from being a total embarrassed joke."

"Yay," I say as she places the tassel into the empty clue box.

"And this"—she shows us a piece of tissue with something wadded up inside of it—"is the piece of gum I was chewing—"

"Ewww!" Rose interjects. "That's disgusting, Al."

"Hold on," she says. "It was the piece of gum I was chewing when I got my period on the pitcher's mound and you guys rescued me for the second time this summer. So I truly believe this piece of gum has sufficient sentimental value to qualify." She looks at me and I nod.

"Okay," Rose concedes, too.

Ally drops the piece of gum into the clue box beside the tassel.

"Thanks, Ally," I say. "It's perfect." Then I turn to Rose.

She pulls open the top of her canvas bag and reaches inside. "I have two things, too. First"—she opens her hand—"this small unused stink bomb."

"No way!" I exclaim.

"And you were giving me crap about my gum!" cries Ally.

"Okay. Okay," Rose says. "But this stink bomb is a symbol of our friendship, too. Birdie came with me when I perpetrated my stink bomb crime." She looks at Ally. "And, Al, you didn't."

"I didn't help you," Ally says. "How is this a symbol of our friendship?"

"Because you stood up to me and told me I was wrong. And Bird, you told me I was wrong but did it with me anyway. Both were acts of friendship. Both of you had my back in different ways."

"Okay," I say.

"Yeah, it's good," Ally says to her.

Rose places the stink bomb carefully inside the box, then slips her hand back in the bag. She pulls out the next item, which is tied together with a piece of string. "Did you know that a violin bow is strung with the hair from a horse's tail?" Rose says.

"No, really?" Ally asks.

"Really. This is from my violin bow. To remind me of how you stood by me and Viking-funeraled my violin when I was really mad and needed to get back at my mum. You didn't stop me. You joined me. Even when it was probably wrong."

I smile to myself. I'm glad Rose realizes it was probably wrong.

She places the lock of horse hair into the box and says, "And you want to hear something stupid?"

"Yeah," I say.

"I sort of miss my violin."

"You do not!" I say.

"I actually do. Looks like I'm going to have to be cool with Mum buying me a new one when we get to England. Is that messed up or what?"

"That's freakin' hilarious is what that is," Ally says.

"Yeah, well. What are you going to do?" She smiles at both of us, then asks, "What about you, Bird?"

"Right." I reach into my plastic bag and pull out the mood ring.

"Not the haunted ring!" Ally says.

"It's not haunted. It was Girl Detective's mood ring and I think it belongs back in the clue box. Because—"

"You don't have the knife in there, do you?" Rose asks.

"If you want, I could go get it. Along with some animal bones."

"Funny," Rose says. "Go on."

"Because this ring represents my friends going on this strange journey with me even when you thought it was crazy."

"Oh yeah, it belongs in the box, then," Rose says.

"Yeah, definitely," Ally says, and they both laugh.

"And this." I pull out the Polaroid selfie we took on my birthday. It's of the three of us at my kitchen table when my mom was bringing in my birthday cake. "This was one of my happiest moments this summer. I want this picture to go into our time capsule so that when we open it ten years from now, we'll see how we are now. How we were then. Whatever." I grin. "We'll be reminded of this."

Together, we gaze at the photo, taking it in. Then I place it in the box with the tassel, the chewed gum, the stink bomb, the horse hair, and the haunted ring.

I hold out my hand, palm down, between us. Ally puts her hand on top of mine, then Rose, and we stack all of our hands together. Our eyes search one another's.

"We three friends. Wherever we go," I say and look to Ally.

"Whatever we do and whoever we meet." Ally looks to Rose.

"And whatever land or sea stands between us," Rose says.

"We will always be bound by this time and place," I continue.

"Of our own special island," Ally says.

"Of our own special world," says Rose.

We look at one another, making it sacred, and together we pledge, "Us three forever." Then throw up our hands.

I'm happy and I'm sad. I lock this moment into my heart—the sights, the feelings, the sounds. And even though it's unsaid, I know we're sharing the same secret fear. That a moment like this might never come for us again.

I close the clue box, latch the lid, and place it at the bottom of the hole that Ally dug. I shovel in the loose soil, and we pat it down with our shoes and the back of the shovel.

And I wonder what we'll be like the next time we dig up this box and *Open If We Dare.*

40

THE NEXT day we say good-bye.

What hasn't been sold or given away has been loaded on a moving truck to be shipped to England. My dad offered to drive Rose and her family to the airport, but her mom decided to hire a car to take them instead. She said it would be easier.

So we stand in Rose's front yard, or what will soon be a stranger's front yard, and watch a driver wearing a hat load up Ashcroft luggage into the back of a massive SUV. It's a Monday afternoon but we're all there. My dad, Zora, Ally, me. Even my mom and the General have skipped work to say good-bye. Simon is huddled with Ashley on the other side of the driveway. And Mrs. Ashcroft is orchestrating it all as if she's directing traffic.

Rose hands the driver her carry-on bag and then walks over to Ally and me. We stand there looking at one another while Rose's mom says good-bye to the other parents.

"So," Rose says.

"So, we'll Skype over the weekend," I say.

"Tell you how school went," adds Ally, because Ally and I start middle school in two days. So many changes in so little time.

"I don't start for weeks," Rose says. "What am I going to do there all by myself?" Her face turns splotchy. Her bottom lip quivers.

"Right. Come on, Rose," calls out Mrs. Ashcroft. "Let's go, Simon."

Simon's girlfriend is crying as Simon hugs her one last time. I don't realize that I'm crying, too, until Rose says, "Don't cry, Bird."

"Okay," I say but keep crying anyway. Then we're all crying. Rose hugs Ally. Then she wraps her arms around me. "Guess what?" she says through her tears.

"What?"

"Remember yesterday when I whispered something to Romeo?"

"Yeah."

"I told him to ask you to the sixth-grade dance."

I pull away from her and stare into her traitorous eyes. "You didn't!"

"I did," she says, laughing and crying.

"We have to go, Rose," her mom says from the car.

We hug one another, in the circle that is us, one last time.

"Okay." Rose lets us go, then gives us one more look. "Go have a wonderful life, my awesome Americans," she says. Then she turns and climbs into the car.

As the SUV pulls out of the driveway, Rose waves to us and we wave back. The SUV rounds the curve in front of the house, and India Rose Ashcroft vanishes from our sight. Reluctantly, we stop waving. I look down and realize I've been holding Ally's hand the whole time.

Afterward, Ally goes home with her mom. With school starting, we probably won't see each other until the weekend, either. I still can't imagine going to school without them. I don't know what that will look like.

As we walk home, Zora starts skipping, and even though she's been feeling better, my mom reminds her not to get too excited. I look back at my mom, walking hand-in-hand with my dad, and realize I'm going to tell her about the summer. About the clue box and everything. I want to be the kind of twelve-year-old girl who still talks to her mother.

Zora grabs my hand and I let her. She looks up at me, concerned. "Don't worry, Birdie," she says. "Rose is going to be all right."

I look down at her and grin. And even though I'm not completely sure, I say, "I know, Zora. I know."

When we get home, I run up to my room because I need to be alone. The pancake Polaroid from the day before is sitting on my desk. My mom must have put it there. I take it to my corkboard and pin it on the last remaining space. Standing back, I see that it is complete. Not another place for another picture. Like we're done now. Those same faces, over and over again. With a few Zoras sprinkled in. It's my life up until now. I wonder what comes next.

Lying back on my bed, I hear thunder and think of Rose. I think about how her new life will be so different. I wonder who her new friends will be and if we'll be jealous. I wonder if she'll hold on to her American accent or slowly concede it over time. And mostly I wonder how, in all my life, I'll ever have another friend like her.

I think about Ally and how this year will be so different for her. Without us at her constant side, who will be her new friends? Will I like them? And will they like me? And what about Joey and the middle school baseball team? I'll be at her games and see her on weekends, but I wonder if things will be the same between us.

And finally, I think about me. Who will be my new friends? And will I have any? I haven't told anyone but I've been thinking about joining the middle school drama club. And I wonder if I would do that if Rose and Ally were with me.

I turn over and pick up the book I've left on my bed ever since I brought it home. *I Don't Know Why She Swallowed the Fly* by Emily McAllister. I open to the inscription for the hundredth time and silently read what she wrote to me:

> *To Birdie, the intrepid—*
> *Go forth and be brave*
> *For the world is waiting.*
> *You have much to give,*
> *And so many books to read.*
> *Imagine.*
>
> > *Love,*
> > *Your biggest fan,*
> > *Girl Detective*

Acknowledgments

BIRDIE'S NEIGHBORHOOD is based on the one where I grew up in Atlanta. I drove through it recently and it looked the same, except the hills weren't as steep and the swimming pool not as grand—and oh, my house wasn't there anymore (shocker!). It's now trees and woods to make way for a flood plain. But Birdie's window was my window and it will always be thus in my heart and mind. So thanks to the families and neighbors of Gainsborough who shaped my childhood, some who sprang up again to populate Birdie's world.

To my visionary agent, Susan Hawk, I live in appreciation of you. Thanks for believing in me. You could have gotten into anybody's rickety car, but you got into mine. And that was a very lucky day for me. I'm so happy to be part of the Roost.

To Anna Roberto, my amazing editor, who encouraged me to write what was in my heart. I so appreciate your brilliant insight and kind support. And special thanks to the Feiwel & Friends team—Liz Dresner, Brittany Pearlman, Nancee Adams-Taylor, Matthew Griffin, and Rebekah Wallin.

I stole from many friendships across my life in the writing of this book. So from the bottom of my heart, I thank Alison Bearman, Patty Lorenz, Gail Plummer, Heather Place, Joy Brown, Margaret Anne Smith, Kate McLaughlin, and Lori Bertazzon for gracing me with friendships that have imprinted upon me for life.

Also, my love and gratitude to Kristine Oller, Alicyn Packard, Jen Brehl, Jen Wenzlaff, Marla Maples, Liz Femi, Robert Davis, Amanda Laufer, Karyn Blaylock, Beth Wolfe, Laura Dawson, Kevin Gregg, Tara Reynolds, Marilyn Alauria, Sonya Vai, Loren Kling, Jen McCreary, Rachel Stander, Margaret Eves, Amy Linton, Rick Lee, Jamie Reeves, Frank Izurieta, Chris and Rita Hamilton, and Greg and Glenda Weaver.

I am so grateful to Oren Weintraub for all his support along my journey. And huge thanks to Kim Haavet, Kate Chavers, Angela de Jesus, and Aaron Mendel for . . . you know . . . everything.

To my Writer's Group and friends, Kate MacDonald, Anna Miller, and Margaret Anne Smith. You wonderful, talented women! Our dinners together helped me believe I might actually become a writer someday.

To bookstores! I was especially blessed to have my first book launch at Once Upon a Time Bookstore in Montrose, CA, my southern launch at FoxTale Book Shoppe in Woodstock, GA, and my first hometown signing at Giggle Monkey Toys in Dahlonega, GA. Thanks to Maureen Palacios and Kris Vreeland; Jackie Tanase, Karen Schwettman, and Gary Parkes; and Tammy and John Clower.

Mostly, thanks to my readers. I love visiting schools and talking to kids about reading, writing, and creativity. Your enthusiasm fills me with purpose and joy. And it reminds me that kids are the same everywhere—absolutely awesome! Thanks to all the schools and teachers and librarians for having me. And a big shout-out to the coolest book club on the planet at Lumpkin County Elementary!

To my mom, Anita Middleton, who uses her many superpowers for good, always supporting me and my writing. How did I get so lucky? And to my father, Guy Middleton, who taught me to ride a bike, to ride a horse, to drive a tractor, and practically everything else—thanks for giving me so much to write about! And to my first and forever friends, my sisters, Sally and Lisa, to whom this book is dedicated. My favorite sound is when you laugh.

And of course the biggest thanks to my fella, Pete.